HADLEY-HADLEY
BENSON

HADLEY-HADLEY BENSON

A NOVEL

JODY WIND DURFEE

Covenant Communications, Inc.

Cover image: A Pair of Red Shoes © by Elliot, Elliot; Getty Images.

Cover design copyright © 2013 by Covenant Communications, Inc.

Published by Covenant Communications, Inc.
American Fork, Utah

Printed in the United States of America
First Printing: August 2013

19 18 17 16 15 14 13   10 9 8 7 6 5 4 3 2 1

ISBN-13: 978-1-62108-151-7

CHAPTER 1

IF I'D BEEN FASTER AT PUTTING on my coat and pulling on my helmet, I probably would've made a clean escape on my bike. Dad caught me in the driveway.

"Yeah, I'd love to help," I said as we watched the new neighbors pull up in two U-hauls, followed by a pick-up, an old car, and a mini-van, "but I already made plans to work on my Eagle project with Bucky and Tanner."

"You made a decision?" Dad asked without being able to hide the approval in his voice. Score.

"We're mostly having a planning meeting."

I *had* decided to do an Eagle project and even though it was still technically winter, the sun was out and I could kind of smell spring. My friends and I had decided to go on a bike ride along the river and I'd make sure to mention an idea about my project to them, so, I wasn't completely lying to get out of helping the new neighbors move in.

"Well, I guess Jarom and Brady can help," Dad said. "But come as soon as you can, okay? It looks like it might take a while."

I wasn't the only one who'd noticed all of the overloaded vehicles. "As soon as we're finished I will. Promise," I added, trying to calculate how long I'd need to be gone.

Rolling slowly down the driveway, I took one more glance toward the neighbors. I saw my dad shaking hands with two people who seemed to be the husband and wife then lifting and handing a box to each of my brothers. He picked up a larger box for himself and they all marched into the house like picnic ants. I felt a fleeting stab of guilt knowing my dad and brothers were going to be there for a long time but the guilt was already starting to wane by the time I reached the blacktop. I would've kept going right on down the street if the neighbor's daughter would've stayed in the car.

I was pulled into their driveway like a magnet as she stretched her arms above her head and looked out of the corner of her eye.

"Too far to walk?" she asked.

"I, uh, was going . . ." I pointed down the street. "But I thought I might be able to help."

I was standing there nodding like the bobble head in my uncle's car when my dad came out for another box.

"Jax, I thought you were going to—"

"It looked like you could use some help. I can do that other stuff later."

Dad looked from me to the girl. His eyes squinted almost imperceptibly. "Uh-huh," he said.

I laid my bike on the lawn and moved up the U-haul ramp without looking at either my dad or the girl. Finding an impressive-sized box marked *bathroom*, I lifted it and traipsed into the house, trying not to break a sweat.

I stopped under the archway to their living room and watched some kid about my age rock back and forth over an old pump organ as steadily as the metronome ticking on the bench at his side. His fingers glided easily over the keys and his feet moved up and down rhythmically and relentlessly. He never looked up. I'm not a big fan of organ music, but he seemed better than the lady at church, and everybody said she was a professional. I took a step closer to get a better look at the boy playing. He didn't seem to notice.

"Don't bug him," said a little girl—maybe his sister—while she marched past carrying a pile of blankets. "Hadley's stressed out today."

I nodded and took a step back. *How stressed out could he be,* I thought. His whole family—and there seemed to be a hundred of them, counting the aunts and uncles who'd helped them drive—as well as my dad, my two younger brothers, and I had been unloading their vehicles while Hadley played the organ like he was providing the sound track for the new *Moving the Neighbors* film.

After about my fiftieth load from the truck to the house, I noticed the music had stopped. As I came around the corner carrying a tall box marked *FRAGILE*, I nearly found whether the contents really were fragile. It felt like I'd run into an invisible force field. I tipped my head to see around the box. There he was—the organist, about the same height as the top of the box, holding out his hand like he was waiting for me to shake it.

"Hello, I'm Hadley-Hadley Benson."

CHAPTER 2

"Um, I'm carrying a . . ." I stammered, trying to state the obvious without being rude.

Some girl I couldn't see yelled at me from the other end of the hall. "Just put it down and shake his hand. He won't move until you do."

By the time I looked around the other side of the box, I saw only the back of her. I had to assume it was the girl I'd met outside.

"But . . ." I started. I thought it was ridiculous for me to put down the box in order to shake the kid's hand.

"Trust me," she shouted again from down the hall.

I took a very slow, deep breath.

"It's nice to meet you," I said as politely as I could. "But why don't I put this in the kitchen and then . . ." I stepped to the side, trying to get around him. He stepped with me, still holding his hand out with his elbow tightly at his side, his arm at just the right angle for shaking. I stepped again. So did he.

"Okay, fine," I said, squatting to put the box on the floor. It wasn't easy. My arms felt like soggy noodles from all of the lifting.

I gripped his hand tightly—too tightly. "Hi, I'm Jaxon Quayle."

"Jaxon-Jaxon Quayle," he said, grasping mine just as tightly. "Pleased to meet you. Uh-huh."

His voice was kind of flat and his expression never changed except to cock his head to the right, glance at me, and then look away so quickly I wasn't sure he'd really seen me.

"Jaxon-Jaxon Quayle," he repeated, dropped my hand, stepped around the box, and disappeared.

"Nice to meet you too," I said to nobody. "How retarded," I added under my breath.

"He's not retarded and I told you he wouldn't move." It was the *outside girl*, somehow standing behind me now.

"No, I didn't say *he's* retarded . . ." I said, turning to face her.

Seeing her up close—well, staring really—wow. Even after traveling and hauling stuff in, she looked really good. She had to be the kid's sister. She looked like him only she was different—or maybe he was different. They both had dark hair and dark eyes but she was a little shorter. There was also a difference in the way she stood and how she moved—not as stiff and awkward. Her hair was in a loose ponytail and I don't think she had makeup on. She didn't need it.

"Good, because he's not *retarded*."

"I didn't mean . . ." I didn't know what else to say. But what I *wanted* to ask was: *Then what is wrong with him?* Obviously she was a mind reader.

"Some of the doctors back home said it was Autistic Spectrum Disorder"—she said the last words almost as if she was a doctor—"maybe Asperger's Syndrome, which is part of the spectrum. At first they thought he might have learning disabilities too—until they gave him an IQ test. He's smarter than I am. He's just different," she said.

No kidding, I thought.

"You'll get used to him."

"Hmm." I nodded my head as if I had any idea what she was talking about. What was I supposed to say to that? *Asper what?* I just knew he was weird. I crouched to pick up the box. By the time I stood up, she was gone. This disappearing/reappearing the Benson family did was starting to unnerve me a bit.

The music started again. I'd had enough. Thankfully my family and I left after the rest of the big things were in. Hadley's mom and dad told us thank you about a million times. I don't know how the mom found her cookie sheets in all of those boxes, but she sent us a plate of chocolate chip later that night. They were the best I'd ever eaten.

I didn't see Hadley-Hadley Benson—as he'd called himself—or his sister until three days later at school, right before lunch.

CHAPTER 3

"Hɪ, Jᴀxᴏɴ," sʜᴇ sᴀɪᴅ ᴀs we passed in the hall.

"Hi . . ." I realized I didn't know her first name. She stopped and turned around.

"Do you know where room 32 is?"

I didn't—which was strange, since this was my second year at the school. "Who's the teacher?" I asked.

"Mrs.—" she looked down at the paper she was holding. "Holmes."

She looked up at me, expectantly. Her eyes were almost black and I noticed she had thick, long lashes.

I'd never heard of Mrs. Holmes.

"I'm not sure, but her class is probably down that hall," I pointed toward the short hall that ran behind the office. "Those are the tens." I pointed to the right. "Those are the twenties." I pointed left. "So those must be the thirties. That's all there is, except for the lunchroom and the gym."

"Thanks," she said and walked off toward the thirties hall. I kept watching her until Tanner Fonnesbeck hit me in the arm.

"Do you *know* her?" he asked. "She is so hot!"

I shrugged. "She moved in next door where the Milfords used to live." I said it like I hadn't noticed what she looked like.

"You've gotta introduce me, *today*. I'm your best friend, right?"

He wasn't, really. Bucky Dennison was. But I shrugged again. "Yeah, I will," I said, "if I see her again."

I did see her again, about thirty seconds later. I couldn't really introduce them, though. Why hadn't I asked my mom her name?

"Come *on*." I turned to see Hadley's sister pleading with him. His face was inches from the wall in the commons area, and he wasn't moving. "The lunchroom is over there. I bet they have pizza." She said it in a sing-song way, like she was talking to a little kid. She looped her arm through his. He didn't seem to notice. "Let's go." She tugged gently. "We're going to miss it."

"No pizza," he said. "No pizza. No pizza." People were starting to stare, including me.

"What do you want, then?" she asked.

"Steak."

I would've chuckled if the situation hadn't felt so uncomfortable.

"You know they don't have steak," she said.

He put his forehead against the wall. "There is steak in our own kitchen, our own kitchen in Pickrell, Nebraska."

"We don't live in Nebraska any more. You know that. Quit being so stubborn and let's go see what they have in the cafeteria." She was way more patient than I would've been. Her cheeks were barely pink and she hardly raised her voice. I would've left him standing there, if I hadn't punched him first.

"Who *is* that kid?" Tanner asked.

I was about to answer, but before I could say anything, Rachel Draper stepped between us and held her hand up to the side of her mouth, like that was going to hide anything she said in her loud, gravelly voice.

"It's her brother," she said. "He's retarded or something."

"How do *you* know?" I asked.

"I was waiting in the office for student council meeting this morning when their mother registered them. He's in that special ed class—that class where they're all together all the time, the one with the kitchen, in the hall behind the office."

Mrs. Holmes, room 32. That's why I didn't know where it was.

"That doesn't mean he's retarded," I said. "Lots of other kids go to special ed."

I thought about how his sister said he was smarter than she was, and she seemed smart to me.

"Well there's *something* wrong with him," she said. I had to agree. "He's in special classes and has to have an aid with him all the time."

"He doesn't have an aid with him now," I pointed out. Why was I defending him, anyway?

"That's probably because his sister said she'd take him to lunch. By the way, I'm starving. Let's go," Rachel said.

Since I was the only person the Bensons knew at school, I felt like I should do something to help—but just then Hadley's sister flashed a glare at the growing crowd. Hadley was getting louder, but she talked to him even more calmly than before.

"Come on!" Tanner pushed me from behind.

"Maybe I should—" I began, gesturing toward Hadley and his sister, but Tanner grabbed my wrist and jerked me along with him toward the cafeteria.

I don't know if Hadley and his sister got lunch that day or not. The last thing I heard was Hadley saying very loudly, "Madelyn Kaye Benson, you know better, uh-huh, you know better. Mother has perfectly fine provisions in the freezer at home. She would be delighted to cook for us immediately, immediately she would cook for us. We must go home for lunch."

At least I knew her name after that.

CHAPTER 4

On Saturday, Tanner hocked spit wads at the dartboard in my garage while Bucky Dennison and I worked on my dad's old Varsity road bike from the seventies that we'd found in the shed out back. Ever since my dad said we could have it, Bucky had been bugging me about a fixed-gear conversion—whatever that was. We'd all been driving with our day licenses since we were fourteen—but other than Tanner, whose parents let him drive their big old family van, we were still saving for cars. I already had a bike that did everything I needed it to do until then, but Bucky was sort of a bike doctor. He could swap out some of my bike's parts, touch it up, and make the whole thing better than the original. Besides, he said it'd be worth a lot of money when we were finished—I could sell it and put the money toward the car. He also said it'd help me stay in shape for soccer until somebody bought it. Win-win.

"Do you think she likes me?" Tanner asked after a spit wad hit the wall.

"Who?" I asked.

"You know, your neighbor."

I knew, but I wanted him to work for it. The truth was I'd thought about her trying to get Hadley to eat lunch about a million times.

"She doesn't even know your ugly face exists," Bucky joined in.

"How do you know? You don't even like girls," Tanner said.

"You wish." Bucky stood up and hocked his own spit wad. It landed right in the middle of the board. "Because then you might have a chance once in a while."

Tanner didn't say anything else. He just grabbed a wrench off the floor and worked on a bolt. It slipped and the paint chipped.

When Bucky was a little kid, his ears were too small and he had really buck teeth, but he was always smiling. He'd pretty much looked like a really happy beaver. His real name was Bradley, but he was stuck with the nickname. He got his teeth fixed and his ears finally caught up with the size of his head, and it was true—girls really liked him. Bucky didn't seem to care other than to irritate Tanner.

"Jaxon-Jaxon Quayle. Hello."

We all turned to look toward the open garage door.

"I'm Hadley-Hadley Benson."

There he was with his hand out, waiting to shake ours. He had his T-shirt tucked smoothly into his slightly hiked-up Levis and he was wearing a brown belt with a rectangular silver buckle. His short hair was parted perfectly down the right side and slicked tightly against his head. We looked at him for too long and then at each other. It was my garage, so I had to do something about him standing there. I stood up and shook his hand.

"Hi Hadley," I said.

"Uh-huh. It's nice to see you again. Good neighbors in Burley-Burley, Idaho, not Pickrell, Nebraska."

I nodded. I knew my eyes were open too wide, and I wanted to reach over and wipe the cynical smirk off Tanner's face. "Hey," Bucky said from where he crouched in front of my bike.

Hadley cocked his head, but just enough to look like a bird.

"We're working on my bike," I said lamely, as if it wasn't obvious.

"Yes," Hadley said. "Bikes are my specialty."

I thought playing the organ was his specialty.

"They are?" I didn't know what else to say. Tanner looked bored and it bugged me. He needed to quit staring.

"Yes, my specialty is bikes."

"Do you know what kind this one is?" Bucky asked him, actually sounding interested.

Hadley moved up beside Bucky, so I did too. We were all standing with our backs to the open garage door, looking at my bike like it was an open-heart-surgery patient.

"Yes, uh-huh," Hadley answered.

My shoulders tightened up when he didn't say anything else. "Maybe he doesn't really know," I said under my breath, hoping Bucky would get a clue.

"Well, what is it?" Bucky blurted out.

I shifted uncomfortably, trying to think of a way to change the subject.

"Jaxon Quayle's bike is a 1973, minty, Varsity, male, Schwinn, ten-speed road bike. However, Bradley Dennison from Mrs. Martin's homeroom number twenty-two appears to be altering the true design somewhat."

Tanner's mouth fell open.

"Wow! Awesome," Bucky said. "You're like a bike encyclopedia. Cool. You know about other bikes too?"

Hadley didn't respond. He looked at the concrete and rocked back and forth at the waist, barely moving.

"Tell them, Hadley."

Madelyn Kaye Benson had joined us in my garage. Tanner looked like he might wet his pants and I quickly wiped my hands down the sides of mine. They'd suddenly started to sweat. Hadley glanced up at his sister and then back at the concrete. I think he had a little smile on his face, but it was hard to tell.

"Hi," I said.

"Hi, Jaxon."

As she took a step closer to Hadley, Tanner elbowed me. He motioned with his head toward Madelyn, obviously wanting to be introduced. I ignored him until he elbowed me hard. I shot him a dirty look.

"Madelyn, this is Tanner Fonnesbeck, and this is Bucky Dennison."

"Hi," she said to both of them. "But call me Maddi."

"However," Hadley said. "Her proper given name is Madelyn Kaye Benson—Madelyn after our paternal grandmother."

"Thanks for explaining, Hadley." She turned toward me. "I hope he wasn't bothering you. He runs away from home sometimes." She seemed to say the second part mostly for Hadley's benefit, scolding him with a half smile.

"No problem," I said, nodding my head too vigorously. "It's cool."

"He's awesome," Bucky said. "How does he know bikes like that?"

She grinned with her whole face and I felt myself smile right along with her. I couldn't seem to help it. "Tell them." She nudged Hadley. He hesitated, so she poked him. "Go on," she said.

There was that weird, quick glance again, and then he spoke to the concrete.

"www dot qbike dot com backslash Road Bike backslash Schwinn or any other equally informative web site available," he said.

"He memorizes things," Maddi added with a shrug, and then said to Hadley, "You can't just leave without telling somebody where you're going. We miss you when you're gone. Come on, it's time for lunch," she said as she put her arm around Hadley's shoulders to lead him from the garage. Tanner stepped right in front of them and stuck out his hand, looking a lot like Hadley.

"Nice to meet you," he said, grabbing her hand before she even had it all the way off of Hadley's shoulder.

Awesome, I thought. *We all get to feel awkward except Tanner, who doesn't realize he's being an idiot, and Hadley, who now doesn't seem to realize he is in the same room.*

"Nice to . . . meet you too," Maddi said tactfully with a touch of *please let go of my hand* in her voice. He shook it way too long.

I was irritated for two reasons. One: Tanner was a moron. And two: He had the guts to shake Maddi's hand. I was standing there like the tree we'd cut down in our back yard.

Bucky leaned forward and took hold of Tanner's shoulders like it was nothing. "Okay Tanner, they'd like to leave now."

Tanner nodded his head with a big, cheesy, stupid grin on his face and finally let go. Then I was mad at Bucky too. He always knew what to do without making anybody too uncomfortable.

Maddi looked at her shoes. She glanced at Bucky and was smiling when she looked away. Of course. She put her arm around Hadley again and took a wide step around Tanner.

"Well," Maddi said. "I guess we'd better go now. See you later."

I mumbled some kind of good-bye like everybody else and watched them walk away. In spite of Hadley's stiffness, they seemed to move together easily.

They hadn't quite reached the end of the driveway when Bucky said, "How'd he know what class I'm in?" I shrugged and shook my head. "And the bikes?" He continued. "He's probably like that guy—you know, Rainman."

"He's not a circus act," Maddi called over her shoulder.

I found myself grinning again. *How'd she hear that?*

"Man, she is so hot," Tanner said. Didn't he know how to say anything else? "Did you see her teeth when she smiled at me?" He always noticed people's teeth. His dad was a dentist and Tanner was a nerd, but he was right—Maddi *did* have great teeth.

"What do you mean smiled at *you?*" Bucky said. "You're daft."

Sometimes out of the blue Bucky will say something like *daft*. But I had to agree with him. Bucky and I had had the word on a vocabulary test the week before. Tanner *was* daft.

"Do you think it bothers her that he's like that?" I asked while I watched her walk across the lawn with her arm still around his shoulder. Hadley's arms hung at his sides.

"She doesn't seem like it. I think he's cool," Bucky said like he believed it.

"But weird," Tanner said.

"I bet you don't know *half* the stuff that kid knows," Bucky said.

"Yeah, but . . ." Tanner smirked like he'd rather be anything than Hadley-Hadley Benson.

As usual, I didn't say anything. We stood and watched Maddi and Hadley walk back to their house until they had gone inside. Hadley didn't look at her the whole way, but I did.

CHAPTER 5

"MOM," I CALLED AS SOON as I put my scriptures on the kitchen counter after staying late at church to help clean up. She came in behind me. "Why haven't the Bensons been at church?" I asked. It had been a couple of weeks since they'd moved in, and I thought Hadley or Maddi might be in my class.

"Because they don't go to our church," Mom said.

"They live next door. They're not in another ward," I said with a *duh* in my voice.

"They don't go to our church, Jaxon. They're not LDS."

"Are you serious? They're so nice and they have all those kids."

She gave me *the look*, which meant I'd said something wrong.

"Since when are Mormons the only nice people who have big families?" she asked with one eyebrow raised.

"I didn't mean it like that," I said. "You know, they just seem to fit the mold."

She opened her eyes a little wider, her hands on her hips. "What mold would that be?"

"Never mind," I said, shaking my head. I went to my room.

Weird. For some reason it didn't feel right. This was Burley, Idaho—Utah's border. There were other churches in town, but almost everybody I knew was Mormon, even if they didn't go to church. I wondered if the Bensons went to one of the other churches. I knew they believed in Jesus because I'd carried a gold-framed picture of Him from the moving van to their front room.

I pulled off my tie and lay back on my bed. So far, Maddi and Hadley acted pretty much like all the other people I knew; well, Hadley . . . but still. Why did knowing they weren't Mormons now make me feel uncomfortable somehow? Nothing had really changed.

As soon as word got out that they weren't members of *the church,* there was going to be a big target on the Bensons' collective foreheads. I felt sorry for them. We would definitely be talking about missionary work in family home evening soon.

I got up and walked over to the window. My room felt stale, and airing it out sometimes kept me from having to clean it. I opened the blinds and could see into the Bensons' back yard. There were still patches of snow in the shadowy places. A row of fruit trees ran along the back fence, and I noticed they'd added a swing set and a trampoline where the grass had been cut away for a garden.

If he wouldn't have cocked his head the way he does, I probably wouldn't have noticed him. Hadley sat on a back patio bench just like Mrs. Wells, the choir teacher, required in class. He stared straight ahead, studying the fence like he was watching a movie. I couldn't see anything special, but he stayed like that—focused, not moving. At least I was watching Hadley, not a wooden fence. Somehow that made me feel better.

Maddi came out of a French door leading to the back yard and shared a blanket with Hadley, her arm moving around his shoulder as she sat down beside him. She leaned her head against his and stared with him, very still.

I looked away, suddenly feeling like an intruder, and lifted my hand to close the window and let down the blinds. Hadley stood up abruptly as if he'd remembered something important he'd forgotten to do. Maddi turned toward my window, watching him disappear through the back doors, with a sad smile on her face. I heard the organ start to play and leaned my head against the screen. Maddi turned and looked straight at me. Of all of the cool things I could've done right then, I ducked.

CHAPTER 6

AFTER BEING CAUGHT SPYING, I'D avoided Maddi at school for two whole days.

Sitting on the front steps of the school, I waited for my mom to pick me up; the book I had to read for English was open on my lap. I'd gone to soccer conditioning, and the busses were long gone. I didn't notice Maddi and Hadley come up behind me.

"Hey, Jaxon," Maddi called.

I'm sure I was extra impressive when I jumped like I'd been electrocuted and sent the book crashing at my feet.

"Sorry," she said, reaching for the book and calmly smoothing the pages. "I didn't mean to scare you. I'm glad you're still here. How are you getting home?"

I wished I could figure out how to stop sweating every time I saw her.

"My mom's coming to get me after she drops my brother off at Scouts."

"Do you think she'd mind giving us a ride home?"

She didn't wait for an answer.

"Hadley decided he didn't want to ride the bus today," she continued. "Somebody was sitting in his seat."

For the first time since I'd met them, she seemed a little irritated with him.

"Clearly he was in my seat, Madelyn Kaye Benson," Hadley said. "Clearly there were plenty of other seats he could have chosen."

"Clearly there were plenty of other seats *we* could've chosen too," Maddi said right back.

"But that would not be proper," Hadley said. He rocked at his waist a little harder than usual. "That would be entirely too uncomfortable, entirely."

"It was entirely too uncomfortable being kicked off the bus," Maddi said.

"You got kicked off the bus?" Our bus driver was the most chill guy I knew.

Maddi took a deep breath and tilted her head all the way back. She might have been counting. "Okay, maybe that's exaggerating. After the bus driver reminded us he had a schedule for the fifth time, I finally bribed Hadley to get off the bus so it could leave, and now we don't have a ride home. My mom is helping at some after-school thing with my little sister, and my dad's at work."

"Why didn't the kid just move?"

"He did."

"Then—"

"It was too late," she said. "He'd already messed up the routine, so Hadley refused to sit anywhere."

"Maybe next time the bus driver could save Hadley's seat," I said, trying to be helpful.

"Very good conclusion," Hadley said. "Excellent suggestion."

"He usually does, but there was a sub today. Apparently they forgot to tell him."

"Sorry." What else could I say?

"Usually I don't care, but . . . We're new here, and people don't know him . . ."

I looked at the cracks in the sidewalk.

"Anyway," she continued. "Do you think your mom would mind?"

I lifted my head. "No, she'd be mad if you *didn't* ask her."

She smiled and her shoulders relaxed. "Your mom's really nice," she said.

"Thanks; she's pretty cool, I guess."

Maddi sat down beside me, and Hadley stayed where he was on the top step. All I could think about was how close she was—the smell of her skin or hair or whatever it was that smelled great and the look on her face when she saw me watching them from my bedroom window. The silence that settled in made it worse.

"I wasn't spying on you guys the other day," I said. *Wow. That was the best I could do?* Somehow I couldn't help but be ridiculous around her.

"It's okay," she said, looking down. "Sometimes I forget what he's like for other people."

"Really, it wasn't like that. I just opened the blinds and saw Hadley. I couldn't figure out what could be so interesting about a fence, and then you came out and—"

"Why'd you duck, then?" She looked skeptical.

"Truth?"

"Always."

"I guess I was trying to figure him out and you caught me looking. I felt stupid."

She was silent, and then she smiled. "I've been trying to figure him out my whole life," she said.

"He's older than you, right?"

"By six minutes." I looked at Hadley and then back at her.

"You're twins?"

She nodded.

"Then how come you're—" I stopped myself, but not in time.

"Normal?" She asked.

"I didn't mean—"

"I know," she said. "We're obviously not identical, even though I get that question a lot." She laughed softly, not saying out loud how dumb people can be. "Nobody really knows why he's like he is and I'm like I am. Just lucky, I guess."

I listened for the sarcasm in her voice, but there wasn't any—just a kind of resignation, like it was what it was.

"Sometimes I think he really is the lucky one," she said. "He's smarter than I am at so many things. I have to study my brains out, but he remembers everything the first time. He doesn't just play the organ, you know. He can play the piano and accordion too."

"The accordion?" I said with a laugh, picturing Hadley in those German overall-shorts things. I laughed again.

"Right now he likes the organ best," she continued. "And he gets away with so much more than I do. Sometimes I think he does weird things just because he can." She leaned her back against the step behind us. "But I love him and can't imagine him any other way."

"I yam what I yam, uh-huh. Popeye the Sailor," Hadley said.

"Yup," she said with a chuckle. "I swear nothing gets past him."

I glanced up at him. *Popeye?* I'd almost forgotten he was there. The last time I'd last paid attention, Hadley had moved farther away, playing some imagined musical piece with his fingers against the sides of his pants. I was surprised he'd been listening at all. I hadn't known him very long, but the times I'd been around, it seemed like one minute he might be *there* and the next he'd be off somewhere in his own head or literally *off somewhere*—like away from everybody else. Maddi lifted my book from my lap.

"*The Scarlet Letter*. I read that last year. It's amazing."

"Yeah," I lied. I thought it was boring.

"You like it?" She asked with a tone of suspicion.

"It's okay."

"Hmm."

"What do you mean?" I asked, like she hadn't guessed right.

"Most of the boys in my class back home thought it was boring, at least until they got into it a little farther," she said, opening to the page with my bookmark.

"Well . . . maybe I'm different," I said. *Where did that come from?*

Maddi looked directly into my eyes with her head cocked a little like the way Hadley cocked his. She held my stare just until I was sure I would look away, and then she shrugged.

"Maybe you are and maybe you aren't. I guess we'll see."

Just then my mom pulled up and honked the horn, as if we hadn't noticed the big blue suburban pull up to the curb. Maddi handed back the book and moved toward Hadley. He'd covered his ears and rocked faster than he usually did. Maddi pulled his hands away from his ears and put her arm around him.

"It's okay," she said to him in a soothing voice. "It's just noise."

Mom rolled down the window.

"I'm so sorry," she said, looking worriedly at Hadley. "I didn't mean to startle anybody."

"It's fine," Maddi said, hugging Hadley tighter. "We're tough. Do you think we could get a ride home?"

"Of course," Mom said, nodding.

Hadley calmed down in response to Maddi's touch, and after a few seconds he acted as if there was no problem. He moved down the steps, opened the front passenger door, slid in, and put on his seatbelt.

"Hadley," Maddi said through the still-open door, "why don't you ride in the back with me?"

He didn't even turn his head to acknowledge she'd spoken.

"It's all right, Maddi," Mom said. "Hadley and I have a lot to talk about."

He stayed in the front seat and Maddi and I grabbed door handles on opposite sides of the Suburban. Before either of us had climbed in, somebody yelled from behind.

"Hey, Jaxon!" It was Bucky, running toward us. "Could I catch a ride with you guys? Heather was going to take me home, but cheerleading's not over yet and I don't really want to wait."

When Maddi smiled it was all I could do to say yes.

"Hi, Bradley," Mom said. She always called him by his real name. "Of course you can have a ride. Hop in."

There was a whole additional seat, but Bucky got in and sat right between Maddi and me. I scooted against the door and stared out the window.

"Hey, buddy," Bucky said to Hadley. "What's up? Havin' a good day?"

Hadley didn't respond except to glance quickly in Bucky's direction and slightly nod his head yes.

"High-five," Bucky said, holding his hand up. Hadley seemed to ignore him. "Don't leave me hanging, dude . . . dude, high-five." Hadley's eyes barely shifted toward Bucky, but then he gave a quick, barely committed high-five back. Maddi lifted her eyes like she was surprised and then grinned.

Great.

"Man, I'm beat!" Bucky continued. "Coach Lions pushed us hard in soccer today. I thought I was going to puke."

"You play soccer?" Maddi asked, leaning in.

"I hope so," he answered. "Right now I'm just trying to make the team." He didn't seem to notice how close she was. "Jaxon's the star, though."

"Really," she said, and I wondered what *that* meant.

"Whatever, Bucky's awesome," I said, because he was.

"I do all right. But if Coach wants somebody to show how it's done, he always picks Jax. It's pathetic for the rest of us."

Maddi stared intently as if judging whether I measured up.

What? I wanted to ask. She turned away just before my face turned red like it always does when I'm nervous or upset.

"We'll have to come and watch a game," Maddi said, seemingly finished sizing me up for now. "Hadley, you want to watch a soccer game with me at the high school some time?"

"Of course, Madelyn Kay Benson. Uh-huh. Certainly. Perhaps we could sit in the center section, row two of the bleachers—not too high, though, never too high."

"If the center section, row two is open, we'll sit there," Maddi said.

"But never too high," Hadley said again.

"Never too high," she reassured. "Let us know when the games are. It'd be fun to watch."

"No problem. Do you play sports?" Bucky asked. I realized she was *my* next-door neighbor and I didn't really know anything about her.

"I played soccer for my high school in Nebraska," she answered. "I was going to try out for softball this year, but then we moved."

I was trying to remember when the girls' tryouts were.

"Hey, why don't you try out here?" Bucky said first. "Girls' conditioning starts next week. You should go."

"I was just going to say that!" I blurted, louder than I intended. I felt the color rush up my neck and into my face this time. They all stared for the longest half-second—even my mom glanced at me in the rearview mirror. *Maybe I could jump from the car when we take the next corner.*

"Thanks, maybe I will," Maddi said. "I'll talk to my mom about Hadley getting home from school without me."

Always Hadley. Didn't she hate scheduling her life around him all the time?

We leaned to the left when we turned onto Bucky's street. I grabbed the handle to keep from sliding, but Bucky didn't even try. Maddi laughed when he smashed her against the door.

"Here we are, Bradley," Mom said. She pulled into his driveway and I hurried to open my door so he could get out on my side.

"Thanks for the ride, Sister Quayle," Bucky said. "See you at school tomorrow," he said to the rest of us.

"She likes you," he said in my face as he walked by.

"You mean she likes *you*," I said.

He was almost to his door when he yelled, "Whatever! You're completely *vacuous*!"

Vacuous? What did that mean? If I was going to keep hanging out with him I needed to start carrying around a dictionary.

When I got back in, pulled the door to the Suburban closed, and buckled my seatbelt, Hadley and my mother were having a great time talking to each other.

"I've been listening to you play the organ while I'm out in the yard," Mom said. "You play beautifully. I was wondering if you could give me some ideas about how to improve. I was just asked to play the piano for our children's group at church and I'm a little nervous."

When my mom turned thirty, she'd decided to take piano lessons. I had to admit she was getting pretty good, but she'd been practicing Primary songs so often *I* could probably play them in my sleep—and I'd never had lessons. The only time I'd heard her play for other people was during family home evening.

Hadley assured her he'd be more than willing to assist her, listing several pieces he'd mastered along with their composers, but was careful to point out pianos and organs are "definitely different instruments, definitely, however similar some elements might be."

I was relieved. With them talking in their weird way, I didn't have to think of anything to say. Maddi laid her head back against the seat and closed her eyes. I watched her shoulders relax as she dropped her hands into her lap. I'd actually been thinking about asking her to prom next week, but now, with Bucky. . . . I turned and looked out the window at the passing houses.

When we pulled into the Bensons' driveway, Hadley got out of the car, stepped to Maddi's door, and swung it open like he was her personal chauffeur. He even bowed.

"Thank you, kind sir," Maddi teased. "And thanks for giving us a ride, Mrs. Quayle. I really appreciate it."

"Yes, Miriam-Miriam Quayle, thank you for the ride," Hadley said.

I wondered how he knew my mother's first name. I don't think *I* knew she had one until I was about seven.

"That isn't polite, Hadley," Maddi said quietly.

"I don't mind," my mom said. "Sometimes I feel like my mother-in-law when people call me Mrs. Quayle."

Hadley opened the door to the passenger side and leaned awkwardly across the seat.

"Miriam-Miriam Quayle, the accommodations, including the conversation, were delightful, uh-huh, delightful. Perhaps we can meet again soon." He shook her hand throughout the entire exchange.

Maddi smiled and shook her head gently. She bent forward to look inside. "Let me know how you like the book when you finish," she said.

I nodded and shrugged at the same time. I could've told her right then how I was going to like the book, but now I'd have to find a way to make it sound like it was my favorite without lying.

CHAPTER 7

THE BREEZE OFF OF THE WATER was cold and I could see my breath. The dirt paths had been overtaken by weeds, and quack grass crunched under my feet. The river was my favorite place to run. Other than an old fisherman hanging his pole over the side of his aluminum boat now and then, there were no people so early in the morning, and the lapping at the water's edge set my pace. Being by myself in the crisp air usually helped me concentrate on my breathing and form, but thanks to an early morning chat with my dad, now I could think only about our conversation. I'd heard it all before, but this time it felt different.

The sun still hadn't come up when I'd thrown on my sweats and grabbed my Nikes, so I thought I would be out the door and back before anybody noticed. It was Saturday, and Mom let everybody sleep in an hour more than on school days. Apparently Dad didn't care about the extra time. I was lacing my second shoe when he came out of the French doors to his office.

"Hey, Jax," he said.

"Hi, Dad."

"Glad you're up before I have to leave this morning."

I nodded my head and half smiled. I'd forgotten about his conference in Boise, or I would've waited to get up until after he'd gone.

"I was wondering if we could talk for a minute," he said.

I knew the "man-to-man" he'd been trying to schedule was unavoidable, but I tried to escape anyway.

"Yeah, but could it maybe wait? I was trying to get a run in before—"

"It'll only take a minute. Why don't you sit down?"

I was already sitting. He seemed nervous and started pacing without looking at me. I raced through the past couple of days in my mind. I couldn't think of any major crime I'd committed.

"You've just had a birthday," he began, "and sixteen is a big deal. I know you've had your daytime license for a long time, but now you're able to drive at night too—all the rights and responsibilities. Do you feel like you're ready?"

I nodded. "Yeah, I'm fine."

He nodded. "And you were ordained a priest last week. Are you nervous about blessing the sacrament?"

"Not really," I answered.

"Just take it slowly and you should be all right."

I bobbed my head. I felt like a buoy. What was he really getting at?

"I was wondering about your Eagle project. Need any help?" He asked. "That's all you have left, right?"

"Yeah, I'm on it." I still had no idea what my final project was going to be.

"Good. I noticed Jeff Anderson got his Eagle last week. I saw his picture in the paper."

Jeff was in our ward, but Dad didn't hear them announce it in sacrament meeting last week because he'd been on assignment in another ward as a high councilman. Jeff was a Scout geek. He wasn't even fourteen yet.

"He's impressive," I said without emotion.

Dad paused.

"Is that all?" I asked. "I'd really like to get out there soon."

"Just one more thing. You'll probably want to start dating . . ."

Without even trying, I thought of Maddi. I shook my head, trying to get rid of the image. Who was I kidding?

"Let me finish," he said as if I'd been shaking my head about what he'd said. He stopped pacing, grabbed a chair, and sat across from me. He had tiny beads of sweat on his nose. "Your mom and I thought it'd be a good idea for me to go over a few things with you, so you're clear. Let's start with some basics,"

I knew that if I looked on his desk I'd find the *For the Strength of Youth* pamphlet and my birthday circled on the calendar with the number *sixteen* and the word *interview* penciled in.

"It's a good idea to go on group or double dates," he continued. "And remember to make sure you and the young lady are home on time—especially if you'd like to see her again. It builds trust with her family and ours. And Jax, it's not a good idea to date steadily, either. You tend to get too familiar with each other and then, you know, things can happen."

It was all I could do to not roll my eyes.

"Those feelings are normal and important but only in the Lord's time."

"Dad, I think we've already had this talk," I said.

"I'm just saying," he continued. "Be respectful and keep your hands where they belong. Do I need to spell that out for you?"

I was tempted to say yes, but I cut him some slack. "No, I get it."

"Are you sure?"

"Yeah, I get it," I said more strongly. I moved to go.

"Just one last thing. I know you've probably heard this a million times," he said, "but it's true. You need to date the kinds of girls you want to marry— in the temple."

That's the part that got me. I'm not sure what the pamphlet says for sure, and I wasn't planning on marrying anybody for a long time, but I couldn't help thinking about Maddi. She didn't fit the criteria.

"Oh, and open her door for her too. It's just good manners."

Another nod and then I thought of Hadley opening Maddi's door with a bow, and I chuckled.

"Did I say something funny?" he asked.

"No, it's not that."

"Good, because this is important," he said. He held my gaze until he was convinced I was taking our talk seriously. "Any questions?"

"Nope," I said, but I wasn't so sure.

"All right. It was nice talking with you this morning. You're a good young man, Jaxon."

And then I left. The thing is, I know all the rules. I've been hearing them repeated for years. Dating girls that are members of the Church is a given, like going home teaching and letting your dad do all the talking. But then there was Maddi. She's good and smart and funny and all you have to do is glance at her to see she's good-looking. The problem is she goes to the wrong church.

I started to mentally review my options. Heather Stevenson is LDS and she's gorgeous. But she loves to look at herself in the mirror. In fact, it doesn't even have to be a mirror—it just has to have a reflection. She obviously loves to laugh—even when it isn't funny. You can barely have a conversation without her snorting.

Rachel Draper is in Tanner's ward and she almost always gets the highest score on everything, but she also has something to say about everybody— mostly when she shouldn't and mostly when she knows the person she's talking about can hear. I couldn't see Maddi hurting anybody's feelings on purpose, and I could talk to her about almost anything. She'd know when not to laugh.

Sarah Kemp and Natalie Preston are both in my ward. Sarah's okay except that she's insane. She won't leave me alone. She left me love notes stuck to our family's car—our *family's* car. Mom actually said it was cute—yeah, if you like stalkers. Natalie goes to church every week. She's smart *and* pretty—and her parents have no idea how many times she's needed a designated driver on

Friday nights. Factoring in Church membership, I didn't seem to have a lot of great options right now.

I stopped running. Once when I was about eight I heard my grandma talking to my dad about Aunt Jenny. I remember because Grandma was so upset. She was having a hard time not crying and her voice shook when she talked. I'd never seen her like that. Jenny was getting married at the meetinghouse, by the bishop. I couldn't figure out why it was such a big deal. Church was good, right? Then she said Jenny's fiancé was a Baptist but didn't go to church very often. The only Baptist I knew was John—John the Baptist. He was supposed to be a good guy.

"What happened?" my grandma had asked. "We've always gone to church and have always had family prayer and family home evening. We haven't always been great about scripture study, but we've tried. Jenny was even president of her Laurel class." And then the tears had spilled over. "She knows better!" My grandma had said. She had buried her head when Dad hugged her.

"She's going to do this, Mom," Dad had said. "We just have to love them and set a good example. Maybe he'll come around. He seems okay."

Grandma hadn't responded.

"Mom, Miriam's a convert."

"I know, but she was baptized before you got married. You were sealed in the temple. You're part of our family for eternity. What if I lose Jenny forever?" And then she had sobbed.

At the time, I thought whatever was going on with Aunt Jenny had to be even worse than when my dog Snickers got hit by a car and died—and that was the most terrible thing I'd ever been through. Obviously the whole thing made an impression. But I wasn't planning on marrying Maddi. I just wanted to ask her to a dance. Now my dad's voice was stuck in my head. *"You need to date the kinds of girls you want to marry—in the temple."*

Maddi seemed like the coolest girl I knew. Not one of those other girls would look out for their brother the way Maddi did. It was just a date. At least I'd be able to get to know her better.

I bent over and touched the ground with my fingers to stretch then I stood up and ran hard. I was definitely going to ask Maddi to the dance. I wondered if I needed to find a date for Hadley.

CHAPTER 8

I FLIPPED UP MY TIE so my forehead wouldn't get that mark on it when I rested it on the bench in front of me. Brother Francis was bearing his testimony. Mostly, testimony meeting consisted of the same people saying the same thing every month—and since I'd heard it before and thought they were telling the truth the first time, I barely listened. My mom seemed to worry that my dozing put my eternal salvation in jeopardy, so she poked me in the side to keep me awake.

"I'm listening," I said every time. She poked me because she was jealous. She didn't have a tie, and if she leaned her head against the bench everybody would know.

It was Katelynne Thomas and her mom's turn. They always went up to the microphone at the same time. Katelynne was little and her mom carried her.

"Okay, ready?" Her mom whispered. I didn't even have to look. I knew exactly what was happening. Katelynne buried her face in her mom's shoulder. "Okay honey, go ahead."

Katelynne shook her head. She had long, blond curly hair and it covered her mom's face. "It's all right," her mother whispered a little louder while brushing back the hair. "You can do it."

Another head-shaking, and then Katelynne finally leaned into the microphone.

"I'D LIKE TO BURY . . ." Katelynne yelled while she put her lips on the microphone. It was so loud that ninety-year-old and mostly-deaf Sister Jeppsen who sat at the end of our row almost fell off the bench from fright. Katelynne buried her face again, whimpered, and refused to say another word.

"It takes a lot of courage to bear your testimony," Katelynne's mother began while I mouthed the words with her. My little sister started to giggle and my mom didn't seem to appreciate my antics. She smacked the back of my head just enough to make a point, but not enough to be out of line in sacrament meeting. I knew my mother was grinning even though I kept my head down. I only looked up when Brother Cannon started to sing a hymn for his testimony, barely off pitch. I was doing okay until I looked over at my brother Jarom—then we were both in trouble. Trying to hold it in made it so much worse when it finally erupted. I laughed first, but covered it with a fake cough. Then Jarom snorted. I thought my mom was going to puncture the skin covering my ribs. I was so glad my dad was a high councilman visiting another ward. Ducking farther behind the seat in front of me helped. Jarom slid down too so we couldn't see each other. I took some deep breaths to regain control and then Brother Cannon hit the last note. I could feel my brother shaking three places down.

"Stop it!" My mom whispered as loudly as she could without drawing too many stares. She put her hand on my shoulder and squeezed.

"Okay okay okay," I said. It hurt. I stopped laughing. My tie was still flipped up, and I almost had my head on the bench when my mom started poking my ribs again.

"What? I'm not doing anything," I said. She kept poking. "What?" I whispered louder.

"Hello, I'm Hadley-Hadley Benson."

I lifted my head so fast I hurt my neck.

He stood in front of the microphone in jeans and a T-shirt with a picture of Spiderman on it. He looked down from the podium, just enough to not look directly at the people in the audience.

"Welcome, uh-huh," Hadley began. "Although the previous hymn was performed with thirty-seven incorrect notes in an unusual key, the lyrics were lovely, yes lovely and important. I believe my good friend Miriam-Miriam Quayle—" As soon as Hadley mentioned my mother, the entire ward—other than Brother Adams, who'd fallen asleep on the stand—turned to stare at our family. They all had that look. *You know him?* they asked without speaking. "—uh-huh, Miriam Quayle will have to provide the sheet music for this exceptional hymn and we can discuss its variations and moving quality."

I sat up straighter on the bench like I'd been paying close attention the whole time but I actually wanted to crawl underneath it. I could feel my face turning red and I barely breathed, but my mother never flinched. She gazed adoringly at Hadley, laced her fingers in her lap, and smiled calmly.

Hadley continued. "'How Great Thou Art' is an engaging, traditional, and inspirational hymn by the German pastor Carl Gustaf Boberg about my benevolent friend Jesus, uh-huh, Jesus Christ. I have performed it for Him often, yes, often at my home, for my congregation at New Life Baptist

Church in Beatrice, Nebraska, and my very good friends at Christ Lutheran Church, 1154 South Berry Road, in Pickrell-Pickrell Nebraska. I will play it for Him now and for you, and for my good friend Jaxon-Jaxon Quayle of Burley, Idaho."

My face burned. Couldn't he leave me out of it? After they all checked to see if I'd been duly embarrassed, every eye followed Hadley as he walked to the pipe organ, pulled out the bench, and slipped off his shoes. The bishop didn't even intervene. Were they crazy? Hadley wasn't even a member of the Church! This whole thing had to be sacrilegious. I puffed out my cheeks to keep from screaming *Somebody stop him!*

Hadley clenched and stretched his fingers three times, adjusted some buttons on the organ, and then placed his curved hands over the keys to play. I waited for the lightning strike. The congregation moved collectively to get a better view, rubbernecking like they were watching a gruesome car accident on the freeway. Then Hadley began to play.

I expected the loud blurp our organist was famous for, but instead the notes coming from the pipes were quiet and gentle. I realized I recognized the song. Hadley's hands and feet moved easily in rhythm. I'd heard the song, but never before performed like this. If I hadn't just seen Hadley standing in front of the ward with his Spiderman t-shirt tucked into his jeans, talking like a robot in his weird way, I would've thought he was any other person who had been invited to perform the special musical number during sacrament meeting. And then I would've flipped my tie up and tried to go back to sleep. Instead, I was wide awake. Each time the music swelled, I could feel it in my chest. I sat back and glanced around at the rest of the ward. There were no papers rustling; the old people weren't whispering over the squeals of their hearing aids, and the kids were still. Tears rolled down my mother's cheeks and she didn't try to wipe them away.

There was silence for at least five whole seconds after he finished. He waited stiffly on the bench until someone shifted in their seat and then Hadley stood and walked down the steps, through the aisle, and out the chapel doors. My mom patted my leg. "You'd better make sure he gets home," she whispered.

CHAPTER 9

I WAS HALFWAY DOWN THE block looking for Hadley before I realized he was walking behind me. He'd obviously taken a detour through the building. I stopped to wait for him to catch up. He stopped too.

"No, Hadley," I said. "You're supposed to—" Supposed to what? I wanted to talk to him like I would my youngest brother, but then I heard Maddi's voice in my head. *He's smarter than I am.* Right then I knew Hadley understood exactly what he was doing.

"Can I walk home with you?" I asked.

He rocked forward and backward, forward and backward, and then nodded his head once. If I had blinked at the wrong time I might have missed it.

"Thanks," I said. We walked, Hadley slightly behind in my blind spot. I had to keep turning my head to make sure he was still there.

"How long have you been playing the organ?" I asked. He didn't answer and when I looked behind, I saw him studying the light filtering through the branches as we walked. "Hadley?" I said again after quietly walking beside him for half a block. The jerk of his head was subtle, but his gaze veered toward me, even though he didn't look at me directly. "How long have you been playing the organ?" I asked again.

"Twelve years, five months, and six days," he answered.

"That's a long time."

"Yes, a long time," Hadley said. "But I began playing the piano twelve years, nine months, and seven days ago."

"Even longer," I said. "I think I started playing soccer when I was three."

"Uh-huh, soccer. Perhaps Madelyn Kaye Benson and I will see a game sometime—center section, row two."

"Perhaps," I said with a laugh. "I hope you do. Have you ever watched a soccer game before?"

"Uh-huh, soccer, soccer in Pickrell, Nebraska. Not Cornhusker football. Soccer. James Franklin Benson, fast forward, number forty-one."

"Who's James?" I asked. I ran through all the Benson kids I knew. Other than Hadley and his father, all the Bensons were girls. There was no James.

"James-James Franklin Benson."

"Yeah, I know. His name's James Franklin Benson. But *who* is James? Is he your brother? Your uncle? Your cousin?"

"James Franklin Benson the first," he said. "Brother number one."   ·

"You have an older brother?"

I wondered if James was in college or married. Hadley had stopped walking. We were almost to the corner of our street, but we hadn't made the turn yet. Hadley didn't answer. I faced him and asked again. He rocked forward and backward with one foot slightly in front of the other and played an invisible instrument with his fingers, tapping notes against the front of his thighs, saying nothing.

"Hadley, is James your older brother?"

"Brother number one," he repeated stiffly. "James-James Franklin Benson."

"I know! But is he *your brother*?" I practically shouted. How did Maddi stand it? Why couldn't he just answer? He rocked some more and then slapped at his sides four or five times. I stepped back and tried to calm my voice like I'd heard Maddi calm hers.

"Sorry," I said. "I just want to know if James is your older brother. I thought you were the oldest."

"James Franklin the first, uh-huh, brother number one. Safe in Pickrell-Pickrell, Nebraska."

"He's still in Pickrell then?"

"Safe in Pickrell."

What did that mean—*safe in Pickrell?*

"Why didn't he come to Idaho too?" I felt like I was playing a nightmare version of twenty questions. I was actually getting mad. It wasn't that important. I could ask Maddi, but I wanted one simple answer. "Is he in school? Is he working? Is he married? Hadley!"

He ignored me or maybe he wasn't listening. He continued silently rocking.

"Never mind. Let's just go. Let's go to your house," I said, stalking ahead. Hadley didn't follow, so just like I'd seen Maddi do before, I walked back and barely took hold of his arm, trying to lead him forward. He jerked away from me hard and fast, swinging his arms. I dodged, thinking he might hit me.

"That is entirely improper, Jaxon Quayle!" he yelled. "Uh-huh entirely."

I stepped way back. He began mumbling, bending faster back and forth at his waist, and then he started moving in small, rocking circles. He began hitting the sides of his head with the palm of his hand over and over, mumbling about James the first and Pickrell, Nebraska.

I didn't dare touch him again and wasn't sure whether I should leave him to go get help or wait with him until he calmed down. Church had to be out soon. I watched for my family. But Maddi got there first. As she came around the corner and saw Hadley, I watched her face change from mild concern to a mixture of real worry, anger, and maybe accusation.

"What happened?" she asked as she moved carefully toward Hadley and spoke softly to him. "It's okay. Calm down, Hadley."

"I don't know," I said.

"*Something* happened! What did you do?"

"I didn't *do* anything. I was walking him home from church, trying to have a normal conversation, and he freaked."

"He doesn't just *freak*. You had to say something or do something—and church is the other direction."

I checked to see where I stood. Church was where I thought. And then I realized she meant the little red brick building with the Valley Baptist Church sign out front.

"Not *your* church—mine. I barely touched him to try to get him to walk home and he went crazy."

"You touched him? When he's upset like this?" Her voice was strained like it took all of her self-control not to yell in my face. "Couldn't you see he was already agitated?"

"Yeah, but—"

"*Your* church? What was he doing there?" She looped her arm gently through Hadley's. He didn't even flinch. "It's all right, Hadley. Let's go home." Finally he seemed to relax a little, and then he moved one of his feet followed by the other. When he seemed ready, we all turned the corner toward home.

"Playing the organ," I said.

"What?"

"Yeah, playing the organ, for my whole ward." I thought about it again and as weird as Sunday had been, thinking about Hadley playing made everything seem less tense. "He's really good," I said seriously. "It was awesome."

She squinted her eyes but didn't say anything.

"I was trying to make sure he got home," I said. "I guess I didn't do very well."

She raised one eyebrow as if to say *obviously*, but took a deep breath instead. "Okay, then what happened?"

"We were just talking and then Hadley said something about James Franklin Benson the first."

She dropped her chin and lowered her eyes. "Oh," she said softly.

"I didn't know who he was, so I asked about him, or tried to."

She looked me in the face. "James was our oldest brother."

"I finally started to figure that out," I said. "Wait, *was?*"

"Hadley," Maddi turned to say. "Jaxon didn't know."

Hadley nodded his head. "Didn't know."

Maddi pulled Hadley closer, maybe to make him feel better or maybe to comfort herself.

"James died the year before last," she said.

"Oh," I said, things becoming clearer. "I'm sorry."

She shrugged and we walked quietly until we reached the edge of the Bensons' front yard.

"Can you wait here a minute?" Maddi asked, tipping her head, waiting for my answer. Everything told me to go home. I was spent and I'd developed a habit of making things worse when I got around her or Hadley, but she sounded like she really wanted me to stay.

"Sure," I said.

She led Hadley to their front door and took him inside, probably delivering him to somebody who could take over the "Hadley-watch" for her. She was back out before I could sit on the still-yellow lawn.

"I'm sorry for getting so upset back there," she said.

"It's fine," I said. "I wouldn't have asked about James if I had known."

"I know," she said as she sat down on the grass, pulled her knees up, and rested her chin on them.

Was I supposed to sit by her? "Maybe I'd better go—"

"Hadley was there when James died," she said, staring straight ahead. "They were on the tractor together. We don't know what happened for sure, but by the time my dad found them, James was underneath it and had lost too much blood. Hadley was pretty out of it. He wouldn't tell us what happened, or maybe he couldn't. He was too upset."

I tried to take it all in. Nobody I knew very well had ever died. How would I handle it if it was somebody in my family? My brother? How did Hadley and the rest of the Bensons handle it?

"Hadley almost didn't come to the funeral," she said. "But at the last minute he came out wearing his suit and tie with James's soccer jersey over the top. Not over the top of his shirt—over the top of his suit coat."

I had to laugh a little. Maddi did too but a tear rolled down her cheek at the same time and she wiped it quickly with the back of her hand.

"Hadley and the jersey made the day easier somehow." More tears spilled over.

I stood there, frozen. *Don't cry, don't cry,* I thought. I hated it when girls cried. I hated it when anybody cried, but especially girls. I never knew what I was supposed to say or do. I should have kneeled down and hugged her or said something brilliant to comfort her, but instead I was sweating and probably had dark, wet spots forming under my arms. As shallow as it was, I hoped she didn't look up.

"I miss him a lot," she said.

I nodded my head but she was looking at her feet.

"Sometimes I wish he'd just show up in my room one night when I'm asleep. I'd probably freak out for a minute, but then I think it'd be okay. Do you think that ever happens?"

She looked up, closing one eye to block the sun, seeming to really want an answer. I held my arms closer to my sides.

"I don't know. Maybe," I said.

I could tell right away that wasn't what she wanted to hear.

She stood up.

"I'm sorry," she said. "You probably think I'm crazy. I just thought—well, your missionaries said you guys think families can live together, you know, after." She shook her head. "Never mind. I'm kind of a mess these days." She nodded toward the road. "Your family's coming. I'll see you tomorrow at school." She turned and headed toward her house.

"Wait," I said.

In a split second I thought about all of the lessons I'd had at church and family home evening. I thought about when my grandpa died. I was broken up about it, but during the family prayer, just before they closed the casket, I felt it. I still cried a lot that day, but somehow I knew he was okay and I'd see him again. He was still *there.* I knew her brother was too, but how did I tell Maddi that?

"Yeah," I blurted.

She turned and studied my face.

"I think you're going to see him again."

"Really?" she asked sincerely.

Did I? "Yeah. I think you will," I said. "You talked to the missionaries?"

She shrugged one shoulder. "Heather Stevenson invited me over to her house to meet them. I thought I'd better know what I was getting into around here."

"That's probably smart," I said. That's all I needed. She was talking to the missionaries. She was golden. There was no way she wouldn't know the gospel was true.

My family pulled into our driveway and would start unloading any minute.

"You'd better go," she said with that smile. "And thanks for today."

I nodded and she turned to go again.

"Hey," I called. She stopped.

"Yes?" She asked, as in *what now?*

"I was wondering if you'd," I swear my tongue swelled three sizes all at once, "um, if you'd like to go to prom with me?"

What was I doing?

She hesitated and studied her clenched hands.

"Sorry," she said. "Tanner Fonnesbeck asked me yesterday."

CHAPTER 10

I WAS NOT GOING TO go to the stupid dance, but then Bucky asked Heather Stevenson and they ganged up on me about asking Rachel Draper. They wanted us in their group. I held out until the last minute, but when nobody else asked her and Heather kept saying how Rachel would probably be scarred for life because she wasn't going to her own junior prom, I had a moment of weakness and gave in. I regretted it almost instantly. If I had known how much money it cost, I would've worked harder to find somebody else to ask her. Plus, I didn't want to see Maddi, especially with Tanner.

When the doorbell rang I stuffed my wallet into my pocket, grabbed my jacket off the hanger, and moved down the stairs toward the door.

"Her corsage," my mom called from the kitchen.

"Oh yeah," I said. Another twenty-five bucks I could've put toward buying a car.

"Let me see how you look," she said.

"He's here. I'm going to be late."

"I'll look fast," she said.

I rolled my eyes and walked into the kitchen.

"Wow, don't you look handsome," she said as soon as I walked through the archway. "Wait here. I'm going to get the camera."

"Mom, Bucky's waiting." The doorbell rang again, followed by a fast knock.

"Go get him," she said. "I'll take your picture together."

She was out of the room before I could answer. She already had tons of pictures of me and Bucky. She had a scrapbook obsession and I really didn't think she needed any more. Our dates weren't even with us. It'd look like Bucky and I went to the dance together. I went to the door and opened it.

"She wants to take our picture."

Bucky grinned and stepped into the house. "My mom got me too."

"Stand in front of the fireplace," Mom said as she entered the living room and looked into the viewfinder, holding the camera in front of her. "Move a little closer."

Bucky and I looked at each other and then he grabbed me around the shoulder and smashed his cheek into mine. She clicked. "Perfect. Now do one for real."

"Mom."

"Just one more."

"Come on," Bucky said like I was a two-year-old. "Don't be gwumpy."

"Fine," I said. "Just one more."

We posed, showing almost all of the teeth in our heads.

"One . . . two . . . three." Click. "Thanks. *That* was a good one," she said sarcastically. "Okay, I give up." She rushed up and hugged me. "Have fun tonight." She slipped money into my suit pocket. "Just in case," she whispered, "and remember to be a gentleman."

"Thanks, Mom," I said.

"We'll make you proud." Bucky stood tall and saluted like he was going into battle. "See ya later."

We were fifteen minutes late to Heather's and we still had to wait another twenty. More pictures and then a repeat of the same thing at Rachel's. I had to admit the girls looked good all dressed up, even though Rachel didn't stop talking the whole time we were at her house and Heather smiled too much, looking at herself in every shiny surface. I imagined what Maddi might look like. I couldn't help it.

"Should we go?" I said trying to get the thought out of my mind. I looked at the time on my phone. We had dinner reservations for seven-thirty and it was ten after.

"We have to wait for Tanner," Bucky said.

"Tanner's in our group?" I asked, instantly starting to sweat.

"Yeah. He said he didn't really want to go with Josh and Katelynn and asked if he could go with us. He's bringing the bus."

Katelynn used to be Tanner's girlfriend, and he and Josh weren't exactly friends.

"Why didn't you tell me?" I knew I sounded panicked and the girls were staring.

"I didn't think it was a big deal." He was lying. He knew it would bother me. "Okay, I knew it would be a big deal," he said. "But I didn't want you to make yourself, or me, crazy all week." He patted me hard on the back once. "I was being a good friend."

"Yeah, thanks," I said flatly.

Tanner didn't knock. He just opened Rachel's front door and stuck his head through. "You ready yet?" He yelled loudly, as if he'd been waiting for us.

Bucky held out his bent arm and Heather linked elbows with him. Rachel grabbed the jacket thing that went over her dress and walked out the door in front of me. I was okay with being last.

Maddi was waiting in the front seat of Tanner's huge family van when we got there.

"You look gorgeous," Heather said to her. She did. Then Heather looked at herself in the side-view mirror.

I could tell by the way Rachel lifted one eyebrow and barely touched the seat that she was afraid something was going to wipe onto her dress. I'd seen the bus a lot worse. I think Tanner had actually vacuumed—there were no French fries under my feet.

The bus was really Tanner's family van, but he'd taken it over after they bought a Suburban. He had painted it orange and black during last year's homecoming, since those are our school colors, and he had installed an awesome stereo. It fit more people than anybody else's cars and even though it had terrible gas mileage, Tanner hardly ever paid. You rode in it, you helped pay for gas. After he added the chandelier in the middle, it became the coolest ride in Burley.

Tanner and Maddi weren't the only ones added to our group. Kevin Abbot and Marcie Anderson sat behind the driver's seat. Zach Morelund and Kelsie Biehl shared the seat behind them with Bucky and Heather, and Rachel and I sat on the seat all the way in the back. There was still a lot of space. I thought sitting in the back was perfect but Rachel didn't seem too happy about it.

"I can't see anybody back here," she whined. "You guys have to turn around and talk to us—except you, Tanner. Keep your eyes on the road." Maddi turned around and smiled and everybody else shifted so they could see us better.

Tanner put in a CD and the sub-woofers thumped under our seat. Everybody except Maddi and I yelled over the top of the music. I guess she was still kind of the new girl. She'd answer if somebody asked her a question, and she laughed when something was funny, but other than that she gazed out of the windshield in front of her or at the buildings and houses sliding past outside.

I was happy nobody could read minds, because I was thinking about how great Maddi's hair looked. It wasn't piled on top of her head in one of those fake hairdos. Only the front was pulled up, and the rest of her hair had just the right amount of curl. She didn't wear too much makeup either.

I liked that she never tried too hard. Man, I had to be going crazy. I could only imagine what those guys would say if they knew I was critiquing Maddi's hairstyle.

"Jaxon!"

I heard my name only when Maddi turned suddenly and caught me staring.

"Jaxon!" Rachel called. "What do you think?"

"Huh?" Obviously I'd missed something because every eye was on me; even Tanner watched me from the rearview mirror.

"What do you think? Blond or brunette?" Rachel asked. Maybe they *were* reading my mind. "Blond or brunette? Blond or brunette? Which one?"

"Brunette," I blurted without thinking. Wrong answer.

"Thanks a lot," Rachel retorted with her stiff blond hair stacked like the little pig's house made of straw.

"I don't know," I said trying to save myself. "I just picked one."

"The wrong one," Rachel spurted.

"Hey," Katie said. "I have brown hair."

"Me too," Marcie added.

Maddi didn't say a word. She just grinned and looked back outside.

"Yeah, but he's not your date," Rachel pointed out.

"Ouch," Tanner added.

"Leave him alone," Bucky said. "Jax has always had a deep appreciation for my ruggedly handsome *café au lait coiffure.*"

I reached over the seat and punched him, even though I didn't know what *café au lait* or *coiffure* meant for sure—something to do with hair, I guessed.

Rachel took about three seconds to recover from me saying the wrong thing and then dominated the conversation again. I paid better attention.

"Basketball or football?" *Basketball.*

"Mexican or Chinese food?" *Mexican.*

"Chocolate or vanilla?"

"Chocolate or vanilla what?" I asked.

"Shakes."

"Vanilla," Maddi and I said at the same time. We both smiled and I hurried to recover. "Because you can add whatever you want to it." I saw Maddi nod her head as she turned back toward the window.

I listened until we reached the parking lot for the restaurant. Tanner put the bus in park and hopped out to get Maddi's door. There was no way I could get Rachel's. First of all, we were in the back seat, and besides that, except for Tanner and Maddi, we were all trapped. The doors were on child lock and even though we banged on the windows, Tanner was so wrapped up in crowding Maddi's personal space they were almost to the entrance before he paid attention to her pointing at us. Bucky had already climbed over the front seat and gone through the driver's side door so he could let the rest of us out before Tanner reached the van.

"You are a dolt," Bucky said when Tanner reached us. "Good thing I have super-hero tendencies."

"Yeah, sorry about that," Tanner said while holding the door. The girls slid through ahead of us in a mass. Bucky went behind them and then Tanner. He pushed the door to close it at just the right time so it caught me on the knee. Nobody noticed. They all continued into the restaurant.

My knee hurt so badly I couldn't yell and I really didn't care what I looked like holding it with one hand, hopping on the other foot. What was wrong with me? I said yes to this! I could've stayed home with my parents and saved a lot of money.

By the time the throbbing had dulled enough for me to grab the door handle and limp inside they were already seated. Nobody asked where I'd been.

"Sit on this side so I can talk to Marcie," Rachel said. I did what I was told and those were the last words she said to me for the rest of dinner. I mostly stared out the window—well not *out* the window exactly, but *at* the window. I could see everybody's reflection on my side of the table. Maddi's dress was pink and gauzy, but not too full. It was perfect on her, even though she was sitting next to Tanner, who was chewing crackers with his mouth open.

CHAPTER 11

We each held our pre-planned pose and the camera clicked—couple pictures, then group pictures. I was ready to be done.

"Come on," Rachel said, grabbing my hand. "Let's dance."

I had to admit I was okay at dancing, and the music had been good, but I wasn't really in the mood. My knee still hurt and a slow song played. Rachel laced her fingers behind my neck, so I had to put my arms loosely—very loosely—around her waist. She put her head against my shoulder and a piece of her stiff hair went up my nose. I'm pretty sure she closed her eyes. A few months ago I would've liked almost any girl to dance with her head on my shoulder. Tonight I pretended to trip so she'd lift it.

The next song was hip-hop, and that meant Rachel had to let go. We all moved out of the way to let Zach move to the middle of the floor. He took off his tux jacket, rolled up his sleeves, and started with a slow pop and lock. Then it seemed he was made of rubber. He suddenly arched and then spun onto his head. None of us could move like him, even though we stood around moving to the music, trying to imitate him the best we could.

"Come on," Bucky yelled over the music while pulling me into the middle. "Let's try it all the way."

I had YouTube. I'd never admit it, but I'd tried some of the moves alone in my room. I was pretty good but never thought I'd be dancing in front of my school. Bucky looked ridiculous but since he had so much fun doing it, he was still cool. I watched Zach, trying to get the moves right, and caught Maddi watching me. My hands went cold instantly and my knees stiffened, but I felt better when she had the right kind of smile on her face.

Heather grabbed Maddi and Rachel and pulled them out next to Bucky and me. Maddi wrinkled her nose, shook her head, and pulled back, but Heather won. She put her hands on each of Maddi's shoulders and made her shake to the music. Rachel barely moved, acting bored, while she scoped the room.

Maddi made a face that said she was trying to figure out how much to risk. She looked at everybody dancing around her—even Kevin and Marcie, who never did anything except the back-and-forth two-step. Suddenly Maddi lifted her head with attitude and went for it. She moved her feet like she was dancing in oil. She did a freeze and then started breaking, but without the spinning on the floor. She was amazing. Besides being a really good dancer, I noticed something else about her. She seemed to be having fun—total fun, nothing held back. She even laughed out loud. I realized I'd never seen her like that, without the watch-dog look on her face. Whenever I'd even *thought* about Maddi before now, Hadley'd been standing right by her, like they automatically went together. She'd probably be offended if I said it in front of her, but it was nice to be around her when she wasn't taking care of Hadley.

"Hey," Tanner yelled. "Watch!" We all turned our heads as he ran up the bleachers and moon-walked over to the end. "I saw this on the Internet the other day."

Tanner perched at the edge like he was going to do a flip off the high dive. Several of us, along with the hovering chaperones, yelled, "Wait!" at the same time, but it was too late. Tanner's foot slipped as he was about to launch.

I don't know what he was trying to do, but the dive didn't go well.

Tanner lay in a heap on the floor, not moving. I thought maybe he'd done something to his neck or head. Maddi's face paled. Bucky and I reached him before anybody else and crouched down beside him. His eyes were closed and his face was whiter than his shirt. Somebody stopped the music and the faculty rushed in, telling the rest of us to move back. We stayed as close as we could and I felt a little better when Tanner started to moan, "My arm, my arm." It wasn't really his arm, though. Blood was soaking his shirt and you could see the hump in the middle of his right collarbone. One of the chaperones ran to the garbage can and threw up.

"Compound fracture to the clavicle," Bucky said, and I knew what he meant. Tanner had one destroyed collarbone.

CHAPTER 12

SOMEBODY HAD OBVIOUSLY CALLED 911 and Tanner's parents. His mom and dad got to the school just after the EMTs arrived. We wanted to follow the ambulance to the hospital for support, but Tanner's parents said it would be best if we finished the dance. They'd let us know how he was, they said.

Tanner's mom wanted to ride in the ambulance while his dad followed behind in their car, so they asked if I'd mind driving the bus home. They said they'd get it later. I was glad our group wouldn't have to find separate rides home.

Nobody felt like dancing after Tanner got hurt, so we all went to the van. This time I opened the front passenger door for Rachel, but she asked if it was okay for her to ride in back with the others. She wanted to be able to talk to everybody else. I shrugged and went back to the driver's side. All I needed was a chauffeur hat.

We thought about watching a movie at somebody's house, but couldn't decide which one, so we dropped Bucky and Heather off with Rachel, since his car was at her house, and then took everybody else home. It was barely eleven when we pulled into Maddi's driveway.

"Thanks for the ride," she said as I put the van in park, but she didn't reach for the handle to get out. Maybe she was waiting for me to open it for her. I grabbed the handle on my own door.

"Wait," she said. "Is it okay if we just sit here for a minute?"

I felt my throat tighten a little. "Sure," I said like it was no big deal.

"Just my luck, I finally have a night out by myself," she said. "And the dance ends early. I don't want my dad to think he's been too generous about my curfew."

I knew what she meant. I was supposed to be in by midnight, but I never thought it would be me bringing Maddi home. Even with space between her seat and mine, my hands were clammy. But I was in no rush to go home.

She leaned forward toward the windshield and tilted her head to the side. "Do you ever watch the stars?"

Watch? "Sometimes, I guess." We'd had to find some constellations at Scout camp a couple of years ago.

"I love laying on the trampoline when it's just starting to get dark," she said. "Stars pop out one by one until the sky is full. It's really dark tonight. Look. It makes the stars seem brighter."

I didn't move very quickly.

"No, really. Look." She pointed up.

I couldn't figure out how to lean over to see the stars and make it cool, but there was no way I was going to tell her no. I leaned forward and tipped my head like she had. I could smell her perfume and didn't really care about the stars at first—but when I really looked, the sky was full, and those were only the ones I could see through the windshield.

"Wow," I said, honestly impressed.

"I know."

We watched silently and it felt okay not to talk.

I remembered somebody saying the most faraway stars—the ones you *think* are blinking out there—had already burned out and the light was just barely getting to where we could see it. There was something cool about still being able to see the light even though the thing that had produced the light was gone.

I didn't sit up until she twisted in her seat and pushed her back against the door, pulling her feet up under her dress. I wished I could see her face more clearly.

"Did you have fun tonight?" I asked.

"Yeah," she said. "Well, until Tanner got hurt."

"Yeah, that stinks. I hope he's all right."

"Me too," she said. "Did you have fun?"

"It got better as it went," I admitted. "You're a good dancer."

"So are you."

"Not like you," I said. "Where'd you learn to do that stuff?"

"I took hip-hop in Nebraska," she said. "And I've seen it on YouTube."

I laughed. "Me, too."

"You took hip-hop in Nebraska?"

"No, I meant—"

"I know. I was kidding. *Do* you think Tanner's going to be okay? He looked pretty bad."

"I think so, but I feel sorry for him. He probably won't be able to play baseball and it's his senior year."

"Yeah," she said. "But—" She stopped.

"But what?" I asked.

"Never mind." She shook her head.

"But *what*?" I prompted.

"What I was going to say makes me sound like an insensitive creep and I don't mean it that way."

I waited until she continued.

"Okay," she said. "I feel *really* bad he got hurt—I do. It was awful. But . . . he seems like somebody who might like the attention."

I laughed. She'd nailed it.

"I shouldn't have said that," she added quickly.

"Maybe, but it's true." I said.

"Tanner's really nice," she said. "I just noticed he's—"

"A little over the top?"

She nodded her head.

"Sometimes I say too much. He said he's your best friend."

"We've been friends for a long time, but he's not my best friend."

"Bucky, then?" She asked.

I shrugged. "Yeah."

"I really like him," she said.

"I know," I said. My voice sounded more disappointed than I'd intended. Her saying she liked him bothered me.

"Shouldn't I?" she asked.

"No. You should. Everybody does." I couldn't seem to stop myself from sounding pathetic.

"He's nice," she said a little defensively.

"I know."

"Well, he is," she said.

I nodded. Bucky was one of the coolest people I knew. He was smart and crazy and real and you couldn't help but like him, but right now I didn't want her to agree.

She shook her head, and if I could've seen her face clearly, she was probably rolling her eyes; I would've been.

"I was just saying he seems fun and he's nice to Hadley."

I was nice to Hadley.

"He talks to him like he's a real person," she continued.

"I talk to Hadley."

"I know. I wasn't saying you don't. I just meant . . . never mind," she said.

"What?" I asked. "I do talk to Hadley sometimes. I just don't always know what to say."

"I know," she said, imitating me.

"Okay, but he's not always the easiest person to talk to."

"Maybe you should try harder. He's not three, and he's not stupid. He has feelings, and even if he doesn't show it very well, he knows when somebody doesn't like him."

"I like him," I said. "I just don't know how to deal with him all the time. He's not *like* everybody else."

"*Deal with him?* So what if he's not *like* everybody else. What's wrong with that? The world would probably be a lot better if more people were like Hadley."

Maybe it would and maybe it wouldn't. I knew it'd be a lot weirder.

"What?" She reached up and turned the dome light on. I instantly felt less brave. "You're obviously thinking something."

My head was saying, *Don't answer.* But my mouth didn't listen.

"Maybe," I said.

"Maybe what?" Maddi asked.

"You can really say you've never wished Hadley was . . . *normal?*"

She seemed ready to snap back at me, but instead she held my gaze and narrowed her eyes until I felt like I was in that dream where I'm at school and forgot to wear pants. Why hadn't I just shut up? She was probably going to get out, slam the door, and never talk to me again. I sat up straighter, ready to take it back, tell her I was sorry, when she turned her head toward the window.

"I love Hadley the way he is," she said.

I should've let it go.

"Okay, but that wasn't the question."

She didn't look happy about me pressuring her, but she didn't get out of the van or slap me. Instead, she looked at her hands in her lap and started twisting the ring on her right finger.

"How could I *not* think about it?" she asked. "We're twins. I've had to think about it almost every day of my life but it doesn't change anything. Me wondering what it would be like if Hadley was different—or not different, I guess—doesn't matter and he's still my best friend."

I'd never thought about being best friends with one of my brothers. I was stuck with them and I had to admit that if Bucky was like Hadley, I probably wouldn't know he existed unless he had a hot sister too. Maddi was with her brother almost all the time and she acted like she was cool with it. At first, I'd thought she spent so much time with Hadley because it was her job or because she didn't have a lot of friends yet.

"Even if he's your best friend, you don't ever imagine what it would be like?" I asked. "You know, to have a normal brother?"

"I had a normal brother," she said.

I'd done it again.

"James. Sorry."

"He was great. He was just one of those people."

"What do you mean?" I asked, but then wished I'd let it go. I remembered the last time we talked about James and I really didn't want her to cry again.

She stopped twisting her ring and stared out of the windshield like she was watching a drive-in movie.

"He was the perfect big brother and he was nice to everybody. I'm not saying that just because he died. I would've said it before too."

I nodded and she suddenly sat up straighter, turned toward me, and grinned.

"One time when I was six or seven, a few of his friends came over and caught him playing Barbie with me. They just stood there and stared at him like he was the one wearing a dress instead of Barbie. He didn't even seem to get embarrassed. He just shrugged and said, 'She wanted to play. Here, help me.' Then he handed them pieces of furniture that went to my Barbie playhouse—Barbie *Dream* House, actually—and they all helped until it was set up. After that, I stayed in and pretended Barbie and Ken were married and the boys went out to play basketball in our backyard."

I think my little sister had a Barbie Dream House. I couldn't see myself playing it with her. What if Tanner walked in? No way.

"I didn't have any idea it was weird for them to play Barbie with me until a long time later," she said.

"He sounds cool."

I found myself trying to imagine him—how he looked.

"How did he do with Hadley?" I asked, maybe a little too boldly.

"James got along with everybody."

Just like Bucky, I thought. *No wonder she likes him.*

"But he wasn't as close to Hadley as I am—probably the twin thing. He was as close as Hadley would let him be, though. James was the one who started Hadley on the piano."

"James knew how to play the piano too?"

"Kind of," she said. "The only song he knew was 'Mary Had a Little Lamb.'" She laughed. "We were three, almost four, and Hadley starting pitching a fit. He did that a lot back then. We were at my aunt's house so my cousin and I could get ready for the Junior Miss Rodeo Pageant together."

"Junior Miss Rodeo?" I teased. "Did you win?"

"No, I did not." She paused. "I was first runner-up."

"Well, that's pretty good," I said.

"They pulled our names out of a cowboy hat. Do you want to hear the rest of the story or not?"

"Yeah, I do. Sorry. Hadley was pitching a fit and you were putting on your spurs."

"Ha ha. They were chaps, not spurs," she said, straight-faced. I laughed, picturing her dressed up as four-year-old Madelyn "Tex" Benson. "Anyway, as soon as James started to play their piano, Hadley quit crying. Immediately. James put Hadley's fingers on the keys next to him and Hadley copied him, exactly. Then he wouldn't *stop* playing 'Mary Had a Little Lamb.' I think my mom and dad enrolled him in piano lessons so he'd learn some new songs."

"It worked," I said. "And not just the piano—the organ too; oh, and the accordion." I chuckled. "How'd he start playing that?"

"It's a long story," she said. "But it was our neighbor who ended up teaching him. I think it was the only way Hadley would let him have any peace."

"I've noticed he can be . . . persistent," I said.

"That's an understatement," she said. "One Sunday my parents were in Bible study class and Hadley escaped, again, from the kids' room we were in. He was like Houdini. Almost the whole congregation had joined in the search, and then they heard 'Twinkle, Twinkle, Little Star' being played on the chapel's organ. He'd been fascinated with it for weeks, but since he was too short to reach the foot pedals, his teacher thought he should wait a while to learn. The church organist was Hadley's piano teacher and she thought him running away to play the organ was so cute she started teaching him anyway, minus the foot pedals. After my parents got the pump organ at home, I used to kneel down and push the pedals for him with my hands.

"You know, I've thought about it, and James could've hated it when Hadley and I were born. He was almost five. We were twins and one of us had special needs. Do you know how much time we must have taken?"

I thought about what it took when there was *one* new baby added to our family. I couldn't really imagine two, and I couldn't imagine one like Hadley at all.

"But I don't remember him ever getting really mad at us," she said. "Okay, he did get upset when Hadley and I glued the pages of his Spiderman comic books together."

"Who wouldn't?" I asked.

"You like comic books?"

"Wolverine," I said.

She grinned and nodded. "I think you would've liked James. You have a lot in common. Both soccer players. Both like comic books."

"Both can't play the piano," I added.

"He could play," she said. "'Mary Had a Little Lamb'?"

"Right. I guess I'm a failure then."

"Not a failure," she said. "Just a little *slow* sometimes."

"What do you mean *slow*?"

Before she could answer, the light on her front porch flashed three times.

"Sorry," she said, trying to sound innocent. "That's the signal. Time's up."

I took hold of her arm before she could open the door.

"*Slow?*" I repeated.

"Yes. Slow. One—I try to say something nice about your best friend and you think I *like* him. And two—Do you know how good it would be for all of us if you were friends with Hadley?" She hesitated and then moved a fraction of an inch closer. "And you're too slow to see I think I could like *you* a lot." She sat up straight again. "That's just a few of the reasons, but I have to go in."

The porch light flashed. I didn't even have time for another breath before she lifted the handle, slid out, and slammed the door behind her. I didn't start the van until she was in her house and all the lights were out. Eventually I must have driven home, because when I woke up the next day, my stomach was still in my throat.

CHAPTER 13

I HADN'T SEEN MADDI SINCE the night of the dance. She and Hadley hadn't been at school for two days.

I didn't realize I'd been so obvious looking for her until Bucky said, without me asking, that their great-aunt had died and they'd gone to her funeral in Boise. Heather had told Bucky.

Even though part of me really wanted to see her, another part was afraid I'd end up following her around like a puppy—maybe even become one of those guys that didn't know when to go away. Rachel had made cookies and invited a bunch of us to visit Tanner that day too. He'd ended up having surgery and was going to be out of school for a while. I wasn't sure I could be there with him and Maddi at the same time and know how to act.

I'd played what Maddi had said the night of the dance in my head about a thousand times, maybe more. I felt almost guilty for liking prom night so much, at least the end of it, and it never would've happened if Tanner hadn't gotten hurt. I tried to remember she'd said she *thought* she could like me a lot, not that she *did*. And Tanner could be an idiot sometimes but he was still my friend and I knew he liked her.

After school, everybody that had gone to the dance in Tanner's van except Maddi crowded onto his doorstep and waited for somebody to answer.

"Hi, everyone," Mrs. Fonnesbeck said as she opened the door. "I'm *so* glad you're here. He's bored—" she lifted her hand to the side of her mouth like she was about to tell a secret— "and he's driving me crazy."

"I heard that," Tanner said from what sounded like his family room.

"Only telling the truth," his mom called out in a sing-song voice. "Love you, honey." She turned back to us with a smile. "I'll be in the kitchen if you need me. Tanner's in there."

Rachel led us through an archway, balancing her plate of cookies on two hands like she might be posing for the cover of a cookbook.

"Hey," Tanner said, definitely perking up as he noticed how many of us had come. He relaxed in a dark brown, leather recliner, a fuzzy, navy-blue blanket covering his legs and feet, watching a game show on TV. His shoulder area was bandaged heavily, almost like he could be wearing football pads, and he wore a brace of some kind.

It looked serious.

We all hovered in a sloppy half-circle around him, Rachel and the other girls closest.

"Are those for me?" Tanner asked, eyeing the cookies.

"I made your favorite," Rachel said, handing him the plate. "The kind with mini M&Ms."

"Awesome," he said.

He fumbled with the plate while trying to take off the plastic wrap with one hand.

"Here, let me help you," Rachel said, taking over the task.

"Is it okay if I share?" Tanner asked. "I get the first one, though."

After Tanner took his, Rachel passed the plate around. I had to give her credit. They were good.

Bucky gestured toward Tanner's bandages. "That's rough, man," he said. "Does it hurt a lot?"

"Yeah, how are you feeling?" Rachel asked with a hint of sugary drama. The other girls all echoed similar questions.

I hung back, happy to let everybody else do the talking.

Tanner shifted his weight and winced in answer to their questions. Most of the girls grimaced along with him, and he seemed to notice.

"Only when I move," he said with just enough martyrdom in his voice.

"Is there anything we can do?" Heather asked, crouching beside his chair.

"I'll be okay," Tanner said, seeming to pause for effect. "Well, maybe, if you don't mind, one of you could get me some ice. The medicine I'm taking gives me really bad cotton mouth."

All of the girls other than Rachel, who probably didn't want to miss any juicy details, practically raced to see who'd get the privilege of refilling his glass. He was a pro.

"What did they end up doing?" Bucky asked while sitting down on the edge of the sofa across from Tanner's chair. Kevin and Zach sat down too and seemed more interested in the game than in what Tanner had to say. I stayed standing, almost behind the back of his recliner.

"They put in a plate and some screws," he said. "It's supposed to take a few months to heal, maybe longer."

"But you're coming back to school before then, right?" Rachel asked.

"Yeah, I should be back sometime next week. I'll know more after my next doctor's appointment."

"So no more sports this year," she said with her usual tact.

I wondered how rude it would be for me to answer for him.

Nope, he's going out to pitch a couple of no-hitters tomorrow, I wanted to say.

"Pretty much," Tanner said instead. "Thanks for asking, though."

I smiled at the trace of sarcasm I detected.

Rachel grinned solemnly.

"No sweat," Bucky said. "You'll be back full tilt and then you'll play in college."

"Maybe," Tanner said. "It depends on how everything heals. It's cool, though. I have a lot of other skills to fall back on if baseball doesn't work out."

"Way to stay positive," Rachel said perkily.

"Hey, Jax," Tanner called, lifting his head to find me.

I moved forward.

"My mom said you were the one who drove everybody home after the dance."

I nodded, fighting to keep my expression even. Maybe if I didn't say too much, he wouldn't ask too many questions.

"Thanks for taking care of things," he said. "Maddi and all that. Was she okay?"

"I think so," I said, as if I had dropped her off at the curb and that was it.

"What did she say?" he asked. "Did she have fun?"

"She said she did," I answered. "She felt bad about you getting hurt, though."

"You know it," he said switching to a big cocky grin. "She probably cried herself to sleep worrying about me." He suddenly looked around. "Hey, where is she?" he asked, as if just noticing she hadn't come.

Rachel told him about the funeral before I had a chance to explain.

"That's okay. I'll see her when she gets back," he said. "It's probably killin' her to stay away."

He laughed, and I tried to laugh with him.

CHAPTER 14

I GOT BACK FROM LUNCH with friends early the next day and there was time before the bell rang, so I went to look for Maddi in the cafeteria. Her family was back from Boise and I hoped she might still be sitting in the lunchroom with Hadley—he took forever to eat.

I decided I had to see her, even though I had no idea what I would say. Did I bring up the dance? The talk after? I went through the back door of the lunchroom and scanned it. I wished I was still in third grade and could write her a note.

I like you.

Do you like me?

Circle yes or *no*.

And how did I bring up Tanner?

They were there, and Maddi had her back to me. I stood and watched without her noticing. Maybe I was becoming a stalker like Sarah Kemp.

I'm pretty sure Hadley saw me when he got up to empty his tray. He hurried over to the garbage can and dumped everything—tray, silverware, everything—and then walked over quickly to shake my hand.

"Jaxon-Jaxon Quayle," he said. "Nice to see you, uh-huh, although you have missed Wednesday's lunch of the day—deluxe beef and cheese, green salad, and hot baked rolls. Madelyn and I would have been happy to have you join us. Delighted."

"Yeah, thanks. I was just—"

"Hadley, you're not supposed to put your tray in the garbage," Maddi said, balancing hers while trying to dig his out at the same time. "Come and help me, please."

He stayed where he was, still shaking my hand.

"Hey, Jaxon," she said, as if seeing me was no big deal. She didn't seem nervous at all.

"Hi," I said suddenly feeling stupid for being so stressed out. "Let me help."

I pulled my hand from Hadley's and moved to the garbage can where Maddi stood bending over the edge. I took her tray and looked in. She'd already fished out all of Hadley's stuff.

"Thanks," she said. "I think I have everything, but would you mind staying with Hadley while I go to the bathroom and wash my hands?"

Hadley and I followed as far as the hall outside of the cafeteria doors. I leaned back against the wall and Hadley stood by the doors as if he was an usher at a theater. I was surprised at how many people shook his hand or high-fived as they walked by. I knew some of them pretty well, but most of them I'd just seen around school. They all smiled more when they talked to him and acted like they'd known Hadley his whole life. He introduced every one of them.

"Clint-Clint Hansen, this is my good friend Jaxon-Jaxon Quayle, my next door neighbor at 2173 Miller Way, Burley-Burley Idaho."

Sometimes he'd introduce them to me. I had no idea why he'd switch it up.

"Jaxon-Jaxon Quayle, this is my good friend Tiffany-Tiffany Hines, lab partner in TLC-foods. Uh-huh. Excellent maker of vanilla pudding, no lumps, exceptional."

"Hi Jaxon," they'd say if they knew me, or "nice to meet you, Jaxon," if they didn't. He talked to everybody and called each one of them his friend, but he never looked at them directly for more than a fraction of a second, if at all. It didn't interfere with him knowing who they were, though. Even with the formal introductions, most people didn't seem too bothered by him. My palms were a little sweaty through the whole thing.

I looked down the hall for Maddi and was relieved to see her walking our way.

"You have a lot of friends," I said to him, waiting for her to take over.

"Yes, good friends, good friends in Burley, Idaho."

I nodded my head. I didn't know as many people as he seemed to know and I'd lived in Burley my whole life. I'd wondered how he'd met them all. I guessed he'd met most, if not all, at school. I didn't think I'd seen anybody eat lunch with him other than me and Maddi. And outside of school, I'd never seen him do anything with anybody other than his family. But it's not like I spent all my extra time keeping tabs, so how would I really know?

"Thanks," Maddi said when she reached us.

"No problem," I said. "He's a popular kid."

She shrugged. "Yeah, most people are really nice." She turned her attention to Hadley. "Ready to go to class?" she asked. I didn't know if I was invited, but I moved along with them anyway, Hadley walking ahead, never looking back.

"I think he knows more people than I do," I said. "And you guys didn't move here that long ago."

"I know," she said. "I get nervous when I have to meet somebody new, but Hadley hardly ever does. Maybe because he doesn't have to follow the same rules, you know?"

"What do you mean?"

"Trying to say the right thing and wear the right clothes and listen to the right music. He doesn't worry about any of that. He just does what he does and talks to almost anybody—except if they're too loud. He doesn't like loud.

"We had this gym teacher in Pickrell. He was a really nice guy, but his voice was kind of harsh and it would sort of boom when he taught. He couldn't help it. My mom finally had to get Hadley transferred, mostly for the coach's sake. He acted like this big ol' tough guy but I think it hurt his feelings that Hadley got upset so often in his class. 'Too loud Coach Bowman, too loud, too loud,' he'd say with his ears covered. And forget about it if Coach tried to use the whistle."

"I'll remember that," I said. "Indoor voices."

She smiled.

"Oh," she continued. "Unless we're at soccer games. For some reason he's just fine with the yelling then, and the whistles, as long as our team's winning."

We both laughed easily and then talked about random things right up until Hadley walked straight through his classroom door without saying a word.

"See ya," Maddi called after him with a chuckle. She didn't seem irritated by his lack of response at all. "One minute he's all good friends and hand shaking and the next you might as well be invisible. Just part of the package, I guess." I think she said it as more of an explanation for me than anything. Obviously, she was used to it.

The bell was going to ring soon and as we moved toward the end of the hall where we'd have to split up and go to our separate classes, I took a deep breath and said, "Can I talk to you for a minute?"

She looked puzzled.

"Isn't that what we've been doing?" She asked.

"No, well, yeah, but about something specific."

"Sure," she said in a drawn-out way.

I'd planned on saying something noble like, *Tanner has been my friend for a long time and he really likes you. I think you should give him a chance*, but I couldn't. The words wouldn't come. I thought about him crowding her in the parking lot of the restaurant, and then Maddi and me watching stars together through the windshield of his van.

"Um, how was your aunt's funeral?"

Wow.

"It was . . . sad," she said slowly, squinting just enough to make me wish the ceiling would fall in on me. "But she was my grandma's sister," she continued. "So I wasn't very close to her." She paused, still squinting. "Thanks for asking, though."

"No problem," I said. The first bell rang. "Well, we better get to class. See ya."

That was it. I left her standing in the hall, probably wondering how I could be so smooth.

CHAPTER 15

As soon as I got home, I walked to the fridge, opened the door and stared into it. There was nothing I really wanted to eat, so I grabbed the milk jug, popped off the lid, and moved it up to my mouth.

"Get a glass," Mom said. I don't know how she knew. She had her back to me, reaching to set a mixing bowl on the top shelf. "Any homework?"

"A few problems in math," I said, moving to the cabinet.

"That shouldn't take you too long. Don't forget Young Men tonight."

I was hoping to skip it, even though I kind of wanted to talk to Bucky about the whole Maddi thing. Maybe he could figure out a way for me to redeem myself after looking like such a moron at school.

"I was thinking you could ask Hadley if he wanted to go."

"Mom," I whined. I didn't really want to babysit Hadley tonight, especially when I didn't want to go to Young Men at all. "Maybe he doesn't like golf," I said. "Maybe it's hard for him."

"He said golfing is his specialty."

"You already talked to him about it? Great."

"I had to ask if it was okay with his mom," she said. "I didn't know he was home and he overheard me. Besides, *I* shouldn't have had to ask at all. You said yes too when the missionaries asked for help. You can pick him up at five."

It was the ward "gang up on the new neighbors" plan. I ran my fingers through my hair and thought for sure I'd bump my hand against the *Preach My Gospel* manual she was holding to my head.

"Fine," I said.

"Good. You can take the car over to the church to meet the Young Men tonight."

She knew I didn't think it was fine, but then I could hear Maddi's voice—*it would be good for all of us if you were friends with Hadley.* Maybe it would help improve my image and I might get to see her when I picked him up. I started feeling better about it.

I poured a glass of milk, grabbed my backpack, and headed for my room.

"By the way," I heard her yell from the kitchen. "The missionaries called to see if they could teach the Bensons at our house Sunday."

I was pushing my bedroom door closed with my foot when she sang, "I said ye-es."

I didn't know whether to be nervous or excited. I hadn't asked Maddi any more about how the missionary thing at Heather's had gone, and she hadn't offered any more information. Who knew if that was good news or bad?

It was ten to five when I opened our front door to go get Hadley. Good thing I looked up before I stepped out or Hadley would've been knocked backward off the porch. He was waiting with his toes against the threshold.

"Whoa, Hadley," I said as I took a step back.

"Jaxon-Jaxon Quayle." He shook my hand. "Golfing is my specialty, uh-huh."

"That's what I hear. Ready to go?" I asked as I looked around him, hoping to see Maddi watching him from their front porch. I caught only a glimpse of her as she turned and went inside. Maybe later.

"Ready to go, uh-huh, ready to go with my good friends to the Burley Golf Course in Burley, Idaho."

I loaded some of my dad's old clubs in the trunk while Hadley opened the door and slid into the passenger seat. He was rocking back and forth when I finally pulled out of my driveway.

I honked the horn when we got to Bucky's house. Hadley honked it three more times before Bucky opened the car door and climbed into the back seat.

"Feeling a little impatient today?" Bucky asked before he saw Hadley. "Hey, buddy! Glad you're here. Gonna hit a bucket with us?"

"Yes, hit a bucket, a bucket of balls at Burley Golf Course," Hadley said. "Golfing is my specialty."

He was excited. He'd already said that golfing was his specialty about a thousand times, and we hadn't even met up with the other guys yet.

"I don't doubt it," Bucky said. "Maybe you can give me some pointers. My stroke is pretty weak these days."

"No hooks. No slices. Nice and easy. Nice and easy, up over to the green," Hadley said.

"Exactly," Bucky said. "Nice and easy."

I had a feeling I might get shown up. I liked golf, but it wasn't my specialty. Every time I saw a big, open, green space, I just wanted to kick around a soccer ball.

I showed Hadley where the drinking fountain was in the meetinghouse while everybody called dibs on the bishop's Escalade, so I sat in the back seat of Brother Spencer's 1992 Geo Metro Hatchback next to Clint Dixon and Geoffrey Marshall. Hadley got shotgun.

Clint and Geoff had taught themselves Kung-fu, so they spent the ride to the golf course talking about their new moves. Hadley told our advisor, "Bryan-Bryan Spencer," everything there was to know about golf clubs—the brands, the weights, what they were made of, and how to use them. I stared out the window.

I was out of the car and almost to the clubhouse before I realized Hadley was still waiting by the car with his arms folded tightly in front of him. His head was cocked slightly to the side and the car door was still open.

I started walking back. "Hadley, this way. Come on," I said.

He tipped his head the other way and finally moved toward me. Bucky ran up beside us.

"Putting range or driving range?" he asked.

I didn't know how Hadley would do, but he'd said golf was his specialty and he'd never yet lied about his specialties. Just to be safe and so we could warm up, we headed for the putting range a few yards behind the brick clubhouse, east of the driving range. Geoff, Clint, Brother Spencer, and a few other people I didn't know had already chosen their places.

Just at the edge of the green, Hadley stopped. Should I lead him? Choose the putting spot? Put the club in his hand? I literally scratched my head trying to figure it out when Hadley took the wrong club out of the bag and walked right onto the range. He placed the ball by his feet and took a stance; my whole body tensed. The club was lofted above his shoulder—not the way anyone shot a putt.

"Watch out!" I yelled at the same time Hadley swung, hard. Brother Spencer's eyes were wide as he yelled, "Fore!" It was too late to do any good. A couple of people ducked, but most of them didn't have time to do anything. At least Burley Golf wasn't too crowded on a Tuesday night in March; it could've been a bigger nightmare than it was. Still, the clubhouse took a beating. Geoff's ninja practice paid off when the ball ricocheted off the building and spiraled toward his head. He arched into a turbo backbend just in time for the ball to whoosh through his hair instead of splat against his forehead. Luckily, nobody got hurt.

"Whoa, buddy," Bucky said, once everything had settled. He and I moved toward Hadley with a hand out for protection. "What happened to nice and easy?"

"Nice and easy," Hadley quoted. "Nice and easy over the corn."

Bucky and I looked at each other.

Corn? I mouthed. Bucky shrugged his shoulders and Hadley started to rock back and forth. I didn't think that was a good sign.

"Try it again?" Bucky asked.

"Are you crazy?" I asked through clenched teeth and a smile, as if that would make it harder for Hadley to know what I was saying. People were staring. They probably wondered if we were *all* crazy, but that didn't stop Bucky.

"First of all, you have the wrong club," Bucky said. He tried to take the driver from Hadley, but Hadley wouldn't loosen his grip. Bucky finally let go.

"Okay," he said. "I've never used a driver to putt, but since this is just practice. . . . Here, stand like this," he instructed, showing Hadley how to bend over the club. "And hold it like this," Bucky said while placing Hadley's hands in the right position. "Now, shoot it really nice and easy."

Bucky took a club and swung it back and forth over an imaginary ball. "Practice it with me." Hadley cocked his head like a bird and looked my way as if waiting for me to explain. I pulled a club. Soon all three of us looked like pendulums on clocks—Hadley's a little less consistent than ours but still better than before.

"How's it going, boys?" The bishop had joined us. I bobbed my head, still swinging my club between Bucky and Hadley.

"I think we're getting it," Bucky said. "Ready, Hadley? I'll go first so you can watch, and then you try."

Bucky placed a ball on the ground and shifted his feet, looking back and forth from the hole to the ball until he tapped it with his club. It barely missed.

"Oh, well," he said, looking at Hadley. "You're up." I dropped a ball, showed Hadley where to stand, and the bishop, Bucky, and I stood back. Hadley took his stance.

"Wait," Bucky said. "Other side. Put your club on the other side of the ball. That's right. Now, nice and easy," Bucky repeated. I held my breath.

Hadley pulled his club away from the ball and swung gently, stopping just before he made contact. He did the same thing three more times. "Go ahead," Bucky said. "Hit it."

Then he did. At the last second he switched it up and—WHAM!—right against the clubhouse again.

"Fore!" the bishop yelled just before he got hit in the leg on the rebound. I didn't have time to do anything but duck and cover my head. People weren't as forgiving as before and shouted all kinds of things to let us know how they felt.

"Too loud," Hadley said while covering his ears. "Too loud! Too loud!"

"That went well," I said to Bucky. And Maddi thought me hanging out with Hadley was a good idea. My mom was going to pay. "Come on, Hadley, let's get out of here."

Of course he didn't come when I asked. He was rigid, except for the rocking. Bucky shrugged, lifted the clubs, and patted me on the back. "Good luck," he said. "I'm gonna help the bishop get to the clubhouse."

"Thanks a lot." My face felt hot. "Hadley, come on," I ordered. "Let's go wait in the car." He actually moved forward. Good. I didn't know what we'd do in the car, but it'd be better than having people stare at both of us.

I thought we'd made progress until Hadley came to a dead stop in front of the driving range.

"Nice and easy on the green," Hadley said. "Nice and easy. Golfing is my specialty."

"Yeah, I saw that," I said sarcastically. Somebody needed to tell him golfing was *not* his specialty. "Let's just go."

"Nice and easy. Nice and easy," he said, rocking back and forth even harder.

I wanted to grab him by the arm, yell that he didn't have a choice, and drag him away, but I knew what would happen if I even *touched* him when he was upset. I took a deep breath and blew it out through my mouth.

"Hadley, I don't think it's a good idea for us to cause any more trouble."

"No trouble, Jaxon-Jaxon Quayle, no trouble. Uh-huh, nice and easy over the corn."

"There is no corn! There's not even a green! We're not golfing a real round. It's practice and we're done. We're going to the car," I said and walked toward the parking lot.

He didn't follow. Instead he walked over to Brother Spencer's golf bag and lifted the driver.

I marched back.

"Hadley, you can't just take that," I said. "You need to ask first."

He ignored me.

"It's all right," Brother Spencer said. "Let him try. Just let me get out of the way first."

Hadley already had the ball on the tee, ready to swing, standing on the wrong side of the ball.

"Wait!" I shouted. It finally hit me. He was left-handed. No wonder he kept hitting the ball into the clubhouse. "Like this," I said, situating him the right way. I still looked around to make sure there was nobody too close in case I was wrong, and then I hid behind the tree south of the range with

Brother Spencer. We both tipped our heads so we could see Hadley around the trunk.

He swung. Beautiful. No hooks. No slices. Perfect. The ball must've carried two hundred and fifty yards, maybe two seventy-five.

"Wow," Brother Spencer and I said at the same time.

It had to be a fluke.

"Holy cow!" Bucky shouted while he ran toward us. He'd been watching from the clubhouse where the bishop was sitting with ice on his leg. Bucky, Brother Spencer, and I walked up beside Hadley.

"That was great," I said. "Can you do it again?"

I handed Hadley another ball and he placed it on the tee. "Jaxon-Jaxon Quayle. Uh-huh. Golfing is my specialty," he said.

He positioned himself carefully and swung. I was no expert, but even I could tell it was impressive. The second shot was straight, smooth, and even longer than the first.

"No way!" we all shouted.

By Hadley's fourth or fifth drive, all of the priests, all the leaders, and most of the employees had gathered near the range. Even the bishop had hobbled over.

"Can you measure it?" Bucky asked one of the golf course employees. He shrugged, pulled out a couple of two-way radios, handed one to another employee, and rode a golf cart toward the far end of the range.

"Okay, Hadley, one more time," I said. "That guy's going to see how far you can hit it."

Hadley tipped his head to one side like he does, darted a sneak peek at me, and looked back at the tee. Brother Spencer placed the ball and got out of the way. Hadley lined up and swung.

You would've thought we'd just watched the winning touchdown of the Super Bowl.

"All right!" everybody shouted while staring down the range. "Way to go!"

Clint started to chant, "Hadley, Hadley, Hadley." Everybody joined in.

"Un*dev*iating," Bucky said with awe.

"Awesome," I whispered, amazed.

"How far?" Bucky asked the kid with the radio.

"Hold on. *What?*" He asked into the radio.

Everybody went silent and waited.

"Three hundred and five yards!" the kid shouted.

Everybody erupted again.

"Hadley, that's incredible!" I shouted as I turned toward him with my hand up for a high-five. He wasn't there. "Hadley? Hey, where's Hadley?" The club lay at my feet. I spun around. I couldn't see him. Why had I been so stupid? It had to be the cheering. He hated loud noises. "I can't find Hadley. Anybody see him?"

"Maybe he went back to the car," Clint suggested. We all turned toward the parking lot. We couldn't see him walking and he couldn't have made it all the way there in such a short time.

"The clubhouse," Bucky said. "I'll go look."

Everybody spread out. I headed toward the river at the course's edge. First I checked the restrooms near the driving range. I even opened the girl's door and called his name—nothing. The only other building was a small cinderblock equipment shed. The door was locked. I still banged against it and then shouted for him just in case. He didn't answer. It was a golf course. There was no way he could've made it to the river already, and there wasn't that much to obstruct somebody's view—but if anybody could get lost in five minutes in a mostly open space, it was Hadley. I clenched my jaw and started thinking of every terrible thing that could happen. Just when things had started to feel good with Maddi—what would I say to her if I lost her brother?

"Hadley!" I shouted more loudly, fighting the impulse to run. "Hadley, where are you?" What if he *had* gone to the river? What if he'd fallen in? It was still icy in some parts and I didn't even know if he could swim. "Hadley!"

"Jaxon! Hey, Jax!" It was Bucky. "I found him!" Hadley walked behind him, not really looking at the ground and not really looking ahead either.

"Where was he?" I yelled, running toward them.

"He had to *go*," Bucky said. "You know."

"I checked the restrooms."

"He was in the employees' restroom."

I turned to Hadley and leaned in. "You need to tell me where you're going," I said. He turned his face away. "I was worried." I sounded like my mother.

He dashed his quick look toward me and then seemed to ignore me.

"Hadley, next time tell me where you're going." *Next time.* I'd actually said *next time.* There was never going to be a *next time.*

He jerked his head toward me, but still didn't look me in the eyes. "It is perfectly normal," he said. "Yes perfectly normal to use the restroom at the appropriate time and place, uh-huh, making sure to wash your hands for a full twenty seconds afterward, a full twenty seconds or slightly more."

Bucky, who'd been watching us like a tennis match, busted up.

"He has a point," he said.

"I have a point," Hadley repeated. "Uh-huh, a point."

I stared at him hard but then had to laugh too, but only a little.

"Okay, you're right," I admitted to Hadley. "It's perfectly normal." He wasn't a two-year-old. "Come on. Let's go back to the car and wait." Even though things had turned out all right, I couldn't take any more golf. I started to jog backward. "And by the way, shotgun."

I'd never seen him run before. I almost let him catch me.

"That is entirely unacceptable," he said. "Entirely."

Maybe I'd let him win—next time.

CHAPTER 16

"Jaxon-Jaxon Quayle, my very good golfing buddy," Hadley said with his arm outstretched to shake my hand when he, Maddi, and I met in the hall on the way to our classes the next day. I didn't feel as nervous about seeing her again as I had before. Hadley unclasped my hand and moved his usual five feet ahead.

"You're his new hero," Maddi said. She was grinning easily and there was barely air between our shoulders as we moved in stride with each other.

"It was all him," I said. "He's pretty much a celebrity with the guys from church. They're still talking about him today."

"He was so excited when he got home. He talked about hanging out with his *very good friends from the Burley-Burley Seventh Ward Young Men.*" Her impression of Hadley was dead-on. "And the ice cream after. He loves ice cream."

"Yeah, I know. He wanted the triple, but the bishop limited us to two scoops."

"Pralines and cream?" She asked.

"Yeah, that must be his favorite. He told me all the other flavors were *unacceptable—Jaxon-Jaxon Quayle. Unacceptable.*" My impression wasn't as good as hers.

"He's big on routine. He and my mom always have pralines and cream. I don't think he's ever tasted any other kind. I always try to talk him into another flavor, but he never goes for it."

"I guess he just knows what he likes," I said.

"That's for sure," she said and then half-shouted, "Hadley!" while moving quickly to catch up with him.

He was running his fingers lightly along the lockers—and across the backsides of anybody looking inside of them.

I laughed out loud when Marcie Anderson turned around with a cheesy, sappy expression on her face like she might have thought it was her boyfriend.

She didn't think it was as funny as I did when she realized it was Hadley—and saw me laughing.

"Sorry," Maddi said to her as she hurried past. She hooked Hadley's arm with hers and led him toward the middle of the hall. "You can't do that. It's weird and people don't like it." He barely glanced at her, and as soon as Maddi dropped back to walk with me, Hadley moved straight over to the lockers again, brushing them again with his fingertips. This time, though, he dropped his arm if there was a person in his way.

"That was fun," she said with a forced grin. "I wonder how many times I *haven't* caught him doing things like that."

"Don't worry about it. Most people understand," I said. *Yeah, like me at the golf course?* I thought.

"So how *did* Hadley do golfing?"

"Well," I started. "His putting was a little dicey, but his long drive, wow. How'd he learn to do that?"

"James and my dad," she said, and then laughed, wrinkling her nose. "I don't think Hadley's putted much."

"I kind of guessed that," I said and wondered how the bishop's leg was.

"We didn't have a golf course in Pickrell, so when there was a break from farming, James and my dad used to take turns hitting balls over the corn we'd planted in our garden. They'd stand in our back yard and hit them as hard and as straight as they could."

Up over the corn. Now it made sense.

"One day Hadley took the driver out of James's hand and hit the ball off the tee. He did pretty well, so they showed him how to do it for real, and Hadley started practicing whenever he wasn't playing an instrument or going to school. Soon Hadley could hit almost as far as James." She turned and looked at me. "So he's good, then?"

"More than good," I said. "Some pros don't hit that far or straight. He's amazing. So, did they teach you too?"

"Are you going to sign us up for the carnival if I say yes?"

"Maybe," I said.

"Then no."

"You *can*," I said. "You can probably hit it *farther* than Hadley."

Hadley glanced back at the sound of his name and slowed his pace—one of those paying-attention-when-I-didn't-think-he-was things.

"Madelyn Kaye Benson," he said. "Great drive, uh-huh. No hooks. No slices. Up over the corn. Great drive."

She *was* good. Hadley had said it and I could tell by the look on her face and the color creeping into her cheeks.

"Here's your class, Hadley," she said. "I'll meet you on the steps after school."

"After school, same time, same place, uh-huh," he answered and then walked through the door—Mrs. Holmes, room 32. After Hadley was in his seat, we moved toward Maddi's class.

"What don't you do?" I asked when we were almost to her class. "So far, I know you play soccer, you're a really good dancer, and every guy in school wants to date you. Oh yeah, and you golf."

She didn't say anything, but her face turned even redder. We walked the rest of the way without talking. I smiled when I imagined her and Hadley as little kids trying to hold golf clubs as big as they were.

"Hand springs," she said just outside the door to the lab. "And knitting. Not too great at either of those—or chemistry." She pointed toward the class. "I'm pretty sure I'll never be nicknamed *Madam Curie*."

"Okay," I said with a laugh, "but everything else I said is true."

"That's nice of you to say, but in case you haven't noticed, people aren't rushing to ask me out. The *girls* hardly talk to me—except sometimes Heather. I'm not whining, just pointing out the flaw in your theory."

She acted like she really didn't know that anytime she walked down the hall guys stopped talking and stared. Girls have no idea how scared boys are of them most of the time, especially when they look like Maddi. And girls are always weird when new people move in, especially other girls.

"It's because you're too pretty," I said matter-of-factly, in the same way I might say *your shoes are red* or *it's a nice day outside*. It just spilled out, easily, and I was kind of surprised I didn't feel stressed out about it.

"Thanks?" she asked more than said.

"Just telling the truth." And then there was nothing else to say and it threatened to get awkward. I think we were both glad when the first bell rang.

"I'd better get in there," she said. "I need all the help I can get. See you later."

I had fewer than five minutes to get to class when she turned and took a step through the door.

"Wait," I said.

She stopped and looked over her shoulder.

"Want to go golfing sometime?" I asked.

She tilted her head with a playful smile.

"I don't know, can you take being shown up by a girl?"

"Bring it on," I said. I'd seen Hadley's putting skills. Maybe I had a slight chance.

"How about soccer instead?" she asked, completely changing the stakes. "Saturday?"

"Soccer?" I asked. "This Saturday?" My voice barely cracked. "Yeah, soccer's good."

"Unless you need more time to practice." She lifted her eyebrows, daring me.

"Nope. I'll be fine. Do you want me to try to get a game together, or—" I secretly hoped she'd say *No, just you and me, kicking a ball around, together at the park* in some flirty voice, but I knew if she did I'd probably go into shock.

"Yeah," she said nodding her head. "I haven't played a game just for fun for a long time."

"I'll talk to some people and then let you know what time I'll pick you up."

"Great," she said and disappeared into her class. I actually leaped in the air.

Tanner was leaning against the wall outside Mr. Mortenson's room three doors down and must've seen the whole thing. I'd forgotten he'd come back to school that day.

"Hey," I said, feeling stupid, but too good to worry about it that much. I walked toward him and raised my hand for a high-five. "Want to play soccer Saturday?" I asked, not thinking about his collarbone.

He only glared and then pushed past me, bumping me hard with his good shoulder. It had to hurt him more than me.

"Best friend—yeah, right," he said as he walked into his class.

The tardy bell rang and I was standing alone in the hall with my hand still hanging in the air.

CHAPTER 17

WHEN I STEPPED ONTO THE covered porch, I felt a twinge of guilt as I thought about Tanner ignoring me since he'd heard me and Maddi talking in the hall. But as soon as Maddi opened the door in pink cut-off sweats that fell just above her knees and a white, long-sleeved tee that said *Beatrice Lady Blaze Soccer* on it, I forgot all about him. Her dark hair was pulled up in a loose ponytail and as far as I could tell, the only makeup she had on was mascara. She looked incredible.

"Ready?" I asked, trying to force spit into my nervous, dry mouth.

"Are you?" She asked with a challenge behind her grin.

"Bring it," I said, feeling the jitters already start to melt away with the banter. I couldn't help but smile back.

She stepped over the threshold onto the front porch, trying to pull the door closed with the knob when Hadley appeared out of nowhere from behind, wrenching it from her grasp. He wore a red soccer jersey tucked into blue-and-white striped shorts and white knee socks pulled over his knees. His shoelaces were too long, even with double knots.

"Ready to go Jaxon-Jaxon Quayle. Center section, row two—not too high though, never too high."

I looked from Maddi to Hadley and back again. I couldn't lie. I was hoping to spend the day without either one of us worrying about Hadley.

"Remember?" Maddi said to him. "We had a deal. We're going to practice later in the back yard."

"Yes, in the backyard later," Hadley repeated. "Now, however, spectator sports are my specialty, uh-huh, spectator sports with the very good friends of Jaxon-Jaxon Quayle—center section, row two."

"Hadley . . ." she droned.

"Maybe we can all play later," I said, trying to help. He darted me one of his bird-like glances, just enough to prove he'd heard what I'd suggested and didn't agree.

"Madelyn, Kaye, Benson," Hadley stated as if he was the judge about to hand down a formal sentence. "It's a free country, uh-huh, perfectly free."

She took a deep breath and then blew out in apparent exasperation. "Do you mind?" She asked me quietly as if pretended confidentiality gave me the option of saying *yes, I mind.* "He gets so bored on the weekends and drives my mom crazy. Soccer really isn't his specialty. He won't want to play. He's afraid of being hit by the ball. Hadley makes a great fan, though."

I hesitated. The truth was, I didn't want him to come but I couldn't think of a good reason why he shouldn't. He was right. Other people from school were going to be there, and like he said, it's a free country.

"Okay, but you'd better cheer the loudest for me," I said as enthusiastically as I could.

"Thanks," Maddi said as she reached over and squeezed my hand for an instant. It was almost enough to make it worth it. "You can come, Hadley, but no shotgun."

He didn't even argue. He just ran to the car, opened the door, and slid into the backseat. He had his seatbelt on before Maddi and I left the porch.

There was no need for me to have to think of something interesting to say to keep the ride from becoming awkwardly quiet. Hadley recited soccer trivia all the way to the field.

"Wow, I think word about the game spread," she said, as we rounded the corner.

Cars were parked every which way along the fence line. For some reason my stomach tightened when I noticed Tanner's orange van parked among them. I didn't expect him to show up with his broken collarbone, especially after the way he'd acted at school.

"It's about time you guys got here," Bucky yelled with his ready smile as soon as we got out of the car. Everybody turned to look at the same time as if ordered by a drill sergeant.

People stood in random groups on the grass, and a few people kicked soccer balls around. I didn't see Tanner until Hadley bolted ahead.

"Center section, row two," he said excitedly as if he was finding seats at a sold-out concert instead of a goof-off soccer game. "Excellent seats, uh-huh, excellent seats for cheering fans."

Hadley didn't seem to notice Tanner and his friends sitting a couple of rows up as he found row two and then picked exactly the right spot in the middle of the bench.

"PLAY BALL!" he shouted as soon as he was situated.

Maddi and I looked at each other and grinned.

"You heard what the man said," Bucky announced. "Let's go!"

The energy of all the people and the upcoming soccer game made me either impulsive or brave—maybe both—and I grabbed Maddi's hand and pulled her along to the head of the field where we all divided into teams. I didn't want to let go when Maddi quickly went to the other team, by choice, with a big daring grin plastered on her face.

"It's on," I said as we lined up on field and she kicked off, left, to Bucky. They dribbled back and forth until I stole the ball and kicked hard toward our goal. A kid from my gym class that was on Bucky's team intercepted and passed to Zach, who played it off the side of his foot and shot for the keep. He barely missed.

"No goal!" Hadley shouted from the bleachers, arm outstretched, pointing out the action. "No goal! Perfectly acceptable for the keeper to use hands, uh-huh, hands in the penalty box only."

I chuckled over Hadley's commentary until I saw Tanner nudge the kid next to him and point the same way Hadley had. They must've thought it was funny. When I glanced back at Maddi, it was clear she'd seen them too.

Nobody else had seemed to notice and since Maddi moved into mid-field and lined up to play, I decided to let it go. The goalie punted hard in my direction and the game got serious, fast. She was good. I was quicker but not by much, and she knew how to build an attack with the rest of her team.

"Wahoo!" Hadley stood and cheered whenever Maddi did something exciting—especially against me. "Yes! Yes!" He'd say, pumping his arm with gusto. Tanner was right behind him every time, playing some second-grade game of copycat. I was getting hot and not just from playing soccer.

"Hey!" I shouted. It came out louder than expected and several people jumped. I didn't want to get into it with everybody watching. I just wanted Tanner to stop. He paused and looked. I glared just long enough for him to see that I'd noticed what he was doing and I didn't like it but then I turned to Hadley.

"I thought we had a deal," I said. "You're supposed to be on my side, remember?"

Hadley gave a weird half-chuckle. "Family ties," he said. "Number-one fan of excellent player Madelyn Kaye Benson. Family comes first—always first."

Even with Tanner's daggers, I had to laugh. "You'd better remember I'm your ride home," I said to Hadley. "I'm watching you." I shifted a glance at Tanner and jumped back into the game.

It moved full tilt, both sides seeming evenly matched, unless Bucky *accidentally* tripped the dribbler or gently forced a player from the opposite team out of bounds. Most of the time I dodged him, but not always. Tanner seemed to not be paying as much attention or was at least being less obvious, until I got back at Bucky and pushed him out of bounds just as he shot for a goal.

"Foul!" Hadley dictated from the bleachers, standing with his now familiar point. "Penalty card! Yellow for sure, possibly red. Free kick. Free kick for Bucky Dennison!"

"What? Now you call it? What about *his* fouls?" I argued while trying to get away from Bucky, who had tackled me from behind and made us both fall to the ground, giving Hadley a whole new round of penalties to call.

"Foul! Foul!" he called, gesturing dramatically. "Foul for Jaxon-Jaxon Quayle and also Bucky Dennison! Penalty kicks for all!"

"Get off me!" I said to Bucky, both of us laughing. I finally broke loose and got to my feet. "Where's the ball?"

Maddi held the ball against her but didn't seem to notice me walking toward her to get it. She was staring up the bleachers intently, her face tense. I followed her gaze with mine to see Tanner standing behind Hadley, mocking everything he did—copying every word he said. Why couldn't he just sit down and be quiet? He must not have noticed us watching, or didn't care—or, as usual, liked the attention from his audience. Whichever it was, Tanner was having too much fun. He kept at it even after nearly everybody around him shifted uncomfortably as Hadley turned and looked back in confusion.

Even Bucky coaxed me to intervene with a nod of his head. I walked as nonchalantly as I could off the field and moved up the bleachers.

"Tanner," I called. He'd dropped his hands after Hadley had, but seemed to pay no attention to me, still chuckling. I said his name again in a way that was too hard for him, or anybody else, to ignore. I swallowed hard when there seemed to be a collective pause as, one by one, nearly everybody on the field or watching the game turned to see what was happening. The smile waned on Tanner's face as he stood behind Hadley, looking at me as if I was some annoying heckler who'd just interrupted his comedy routine.

Maddi dropped the ball at Bucky's feet and headed toward the bleachers too. She looked more worried than mad and seemed to keep all of her attention on Hadley. Bucky tried to pull attention away from us and back to the game, but quit when Tanner finally met me in the aisle. Most of the crowd gave up any subtlety, apparently leaning in to hear better.

"Dude, you need to back off," I said with my voice lowered.

"What? I was just joking around," Tanner said too loudly as if he thought it was fine, like he had nothing to hide. I felt my shoulders tense.

"Whatever. It's not cool. People are watching. His sister's over there."

Tanner glanced at Maddi as she made her way up the last few bleachers and reached Hadley. She put her hand on his shoulder, the only one who could when he was upset, and tried to guide him farther down the aisle, away from us. Hadley was resisting.

Tanner looked back at me, his face turning harder. "His sister—yeah, right. You mean *your girlfriend*."

He leaned forward challengingly, puffing his nasty breath in my face. Shoulder brace or not, I wanted to shove him out of my space, let him know how out of line I thought he was, but instead I half laughed, took a step back, and shook my head.

Suddenly he seemed pathetic.

My girlfriend? Is that what this was about? If only.

"I can't imagine *why* she's not falling all over you," I said, darting a quick glance at Hadley to make my point.

His face burned hot.

"You know what?" he asked, even more loudly but with a kind of controlled boil. "I'm sick of you acting like the hero of the universe. If his sister didn't look like that, you wouldn't even know that kid existed!" And with the last word he pushed me in the shoulder with his free hand. Normally the shove would've only made me sway a little, but my heels were too near the edge of the bleacher step and I teetered backward, swinging my arms to gain balance. I twisted hard and buckled my knees at the right time to stop from toppling more than a couple of steps. I hardly felt the raw, burning scrapes but stood almost as soon as I'd fallen. I wadded Tanner's shirt in one hand, my other balled up next to his face. My whole body shook, I wanted to pound into him so badly. I hadn't noticed Hadley had broken away from Maddi until he stepped into view, his face inches from Tanner's and mine.

"Indira," he said evenly. "Indira Ghandi."

Tanner's scrunched-up face and my tensed hand relaxed narrowly as we both turned our heads Hadley's way at the same time.

"*What?*" we echoed.

"Mrs. Ghandi, uh-huh, Mrs. Indira Ghandi said: *You can't shake hands with a clenched fist.* No clenched fists. Have to shake on it only. Friends shake hands—good friends like Tanner Fonnesbeck and Jaxon-Jaxon Quayle."

I glanced rigidly from Hadley to Maddi, who'd moved next to her brother. My stiff hand was still suspended. Hadley's head was tilted, his gaze not quite settled on mine. A helpless grin formed on Maddi's lips and she shrugged.

"I'm pretty sure that's the exact quote," she said.

My heart was still pounding with adrenaline, but after Hadley's *You can't shake hands with a clenched fist* and Maddi's calm, cool, and collected persona, I knew I couldn't hit Tanner.

I took a deep breath and then swallowed hard. Slowly, I forced myself to let go of Tanner's crumpled shirt. I dropped both of my hands until I lifted my arm to a ninety-degree angle—Hadley style.

"Have to shake on it," I repeated tightly.

Tanner stared at my open hand for what seemed like forever with everybody looking on. Finally he slapped it away.

"Let's go," he said to the group he'd been sitting with and he trudged down the bleachers, not looking back to see if any of them followed. It was as if the whole crowd watched him in unison until he climbed inside the driver's seat of his van, started it, and then sped away.

"You guys finished already?" Bucky shouted from the field "I'm about to be resplendent down here!"

Resplendent. I shook my head and, with the rest of the crowd, let my shoulders relax. "Thanks," Maddi said softly, her eyes smiling as she slipped her hand in mine.

I shrugged one shoulder as if butterflies hadn't suddenly assaulted my insides. "Center section, row two?" I asked Hadley.

"Never too high," he added nervously, seeming to realize for the first time he'd moved to row five or six. "Never too high."

CHAPTER 18

I THOUGHT WE SHOULD HAVE a barbecue and eat outside—lay out blankets picnic-style for the kids and use lawn chairs for the older people. The weather was great, it'd be a lot less stressful to get ready for, there would hardly be any mess to clean up, and it would be way more relaxed. But my mother wouldn't listen.

"This could be one of the most important nights of the Bensons' lives, even if they don't know it yet," Mom said.

I reminded her that Maddi had taken a few missionary discussions at Heather's, so the whole thing wasn't exactly new. She just handed me a stack of china plates and turned me toward the dining room.

Between the Benson family and mine, we used our regular table with both leaves, two card tables pushed together for the littler kids, and all three stools up to the island in the kitchen. The missionaries were coming after dinner. I guess there's some unofficial idea suggesting it's best for the investigators and their contact family to spend some time together before the missionaries get there.

Noise and chaos was the only way to describe the gathering. Dad sat at the head of the table as usual, most of the little kids sat around the card tables, and the rest of us scrambled for whatever seat we could get. It seemed to take forever before we were all quiet enough to pray.

During the passing of the food, it only took about five seconds for my little sister, the only one not at the kids' table, to knock her drink into Mr. Benson's lap. My brother demonstrated how he could squish his chewed-up peas through the gap in his front teeth and sprayed them all over Chloe, the Bensons' youngest, at the same time. She'd leaned in to study his technique.

Both of my parents apologized profusely. "Don't worry about it," Mr. and Mrs. Benson both said. "Really." They tried as discreetly as possible to soak up the spot on Mr. Benson's pants with extra napkins and to wipe the recycled peas from Chloe's scrunched-up face.

"Kids," Mr. Benson shrugged easily.

I'd been nervous about the missionaries coming over, thinking the Bensons were probably too polite to tell my family to back off. Now I wondered if they'd even stay for the rest of dinner.

"And we're using our *best* manners tonight," I said to Maddi, who was sitting across the table from me, using as much sarcasm as I could conjure. "Yep, my family's impressive."

Maddi only grinned and then pushed peas through her perfectly straight front teeth with great skill.

"Works with the mashed potatoes too," she said after swallowing. It was a lot cuter than when my brother did it.

By some miracle, the Bensons still sat in our living room when the missionaries knocked on our front door. Kids were on the floor playing games, Dad was talking to Mr. Benson about the economy, Mom was chatting with Mrs. Benson about I don't know what, and Hadley was playing hymns on the piano. His mom had insisted on the quiet pedal.

Maddi and I sat with our backs against the couch looking at photo albums my mom had conveniently left next to several sets of scriptures on the coffee table. I have to admit, everybody seemed relaxed. It probably helped that my mom had outdone herself, even with the typical roast beef and mashed potatoes, and Mrs. Benson's Dutch oven cherry cobbler—which was forbidden until the missionaries got there—smelled fantastic.

When the missionaries stepped across the threshold and into the entry, we all shifted into an imperfect circle around the room, leaving them space to sit at the head. I read their tags: Elder Call and Elder Forsgren. The missionaries shook everybody's hand—quite an accomplishment considering how many of us there were and how enthusiastic Hadley was about handshaking—and everyone was introduced.

"Do you mind if we start with a word of prayer?" Elder Call asked once he and his companion were finally seated. "Brother Quayle, this is your home; would you like to call on somebody?"

I could feel it before he said my name.

"Jaxon?"

In front of all these people? I'd never prayed for something like this before. What was I supposed to say? I took a quick breath and bowed my head. Generic. Thank you we could all be here. Thank you for the gospel. Please bless us to do what's right. Please help us listen to the missionaries. I opened one eye to a slit when Mrs. Benson said an audible *amen* to that. Then I closed in the name of Jesus Christ and said my own *amen.*

"Thank you, Jaxon," my dad said and then turned the rest of the time over to the missionaries. Both held the scriptures and one had a copy of *Preach My Gospel*.

"Maddi," Elder Call said, "we know you've heard some of the things we'd like to talk about tonight when we met with you at Heather's, but we think it's important for your family to hear them too. Hopefully you won't be too bored. Jump in if you have anything to add. That goes for the rest of you as well, and we'll try to answer any questions you have."

The lesson was basically the same one I'd heard at church and seminary a thousand times or more. It was hard to pay attention, like listening to the same song over and over on the radio—except for the expressions on the Bensons' faces. They were taking in every word. Hadley looked directly at the missionaries a few times and even the little kids seemed to pay attention. It made me wonder how this would all sound for the first time.

It was clear the Bensons knew the Bible. Hadley quoted several scriptures, mostly backing up what the elders taught about Heavenly Father and Jesus. Mrs. Benson nodded her head with the same *amen* she'd uttered earlier, and even Mr. Benson, who was serious and seemed the most guarded, sat forward with interest about the idea that the apostasy required a restoration, not a reformation. Everybody agreed that living by the teachings of Jesus Christ strengthened families.

I was worried about the Joseph Smith part. That's where I was afraid they'd get tripped up, but they didn't seem to think it was too weird. Maybe out of respect, one of the younger Benson girls—Rachel, I think—brought up King David and Samuel from the Old Testament.

"Very young also," Hadley agreed. "Very young to talk with God."

I'd never thought of that before. I was impressed Rachel even knew who they were. I was probably in seventh or eighth grade before I knew anything more about David than the fact that he'd killed a giant, which I thought was very cool. And until recently the only Samuel I knew was Samuel the Lamanite, the Superman of the Book of Mormon—impervious to weapons. Maddi said nothing the whole time, her face mostly unreadable. I couldn't tell if she was feeling it or not. I think Elder Call was comparing the Quorum of the Twelve during ancient times and now when out of nowhere Maddi asked, "What about my brother James?"

The room was instantly still except for Hadley quietly repeating, "James-James Franklin Benson the first," as if he'd been thinking the same thing as Maddi.

"What do you mean?" Elder Call asked.

Maddi breathed in slowly and deeply, like she was trying to decide what to say. A crease formed between her eyes.

"James died and when we were at Heather's you said if we followed the commandments and did what we needed to do, we could live together forever as a family." She darted a quick look at her mother, whose hands were laced tightly in her lap. Her eyes were sad.

"That's right," Elder Call affirmed. "We can. There are some things you have to do, like be baptized and work with your bishop to prepare to go to the temple and be sealed as a family. But if you do those things and then live the gospel the best way you know how, your family can live together forever."

"But he's not here anymore. How can he be a part of any of that? If this is all true—" Maddi stressed the word *if*—"then does that mean he's left out? We will be together in heaven minus James?"

The two elders exchanged an understanding look. Elder Call gave the floor to Elder Forsgren.

"You've jumped ahead a little," he said with a smile. "But I think we should talk about it now. Would you please turn with me to 1 Corinthians, chapter 15, verse 29 in the New Testament?" My mom passed various sets of scriptures around the room, starting with Mr. and Mrs. Benson.

I was curious about where he was going, so I opened my own scriptures, which up until then had been closed in my lap. Maddi and I shared.

"Would you mind reading?" Elder Forsgren asked Maddi.

I followed along silently.

"Else what shall they do which are baptized for the dead. If the dead rise not at all? Why are they then baptized for the dead?" Maddi paused, leaving her eyes on the page until she raised her chin. "Do you mean he can still be baptized? How?"

I tried to imagine what they were thinking—tried to see it from their points of view. If it wasn't explained correctly, I thought it could all seem confusing and even a little creepy.

"He can," Elder Forsgren said. "God loves all of His children and through the Restoration we talked about earlier, He's made it possible for those who didn't get to hear the gospel in this life to hear about it in the next. Temple work, which includes baptism for the dead, can be done by proxy." He turned to the younger kids. "Does anybody know what *proxy* means?"

"Proxy. Noun. A person authorized to act for another. Uh-huh one for the other—like Jesus and the Resurrection," Hadley said.

"Excellent point, Hadley. Thanks," Elder Forsgren said.

"Wait a minute," Mr. Benson interrupted. He quickly scanned the scripture again. "I've read this before, but I didn't know what it meant exactly. I figured it was something they did back in Jesus's day, not now."

"They did do it in Jesus's day," Elder Call interjected matter-of-factly.

"Yes," Mr. Benson said. "But now you're saying that somebody can be baptized into your church for somebody else, at *this* time?"

"Yes, sir," Elder Forsgren said.

"No disrespect, but what if the person being baptized by proxy has no desire to be a member of your church? Like Hadley said—authorized by who?" Mr. Benson's voice was even but there seemed to be a new tightness in the room. I glanced around, hoping for somebody to break the tension.

"Maybe I can answer that," my dad said. "My grandfather wasn't a member of our church, but my wife and I went ahead and did his temple work, which includes baptism for the dead, a few years ago, several years after he passed. If he's still anything like he was on earth, I imagine he could be . . . reluctant, to say the least, but we wanted to give him the chance to accept it if he would. What I'm trying to say is, the person always has a choice. Agency is still a working principle, no matter where we are in the scheme of things."

Mr. Benson nodded slowly, acting like he was trying to take it all in, but not completely convinced.

"James knows," Hadley said. "James Franklin Benson the first, willing and able."

"We don't know that, Hadley," Maddi stated.

"But if it's true . . ." Mrs. Benson said.

"We need to know a lot more before we could even begin to think like that," Mr. Benson asserted.

"I agree," Elder Forsgren said. "We've given you a lot to think about tonight. A lot more than we planned. What we've discussed is either true or it isn't; if you pray to God and ask with sincerity, you can know for yourselves. Will you agree to do that?"

"*Let him ask of God.* Uh-huh. James-James chapter 1, verse 5," Hadley said. "James Franklin Benson the first."

I shifted my gaze to Maddi and was surprised to find her looking back at me, the same intensity still there. *What? Say yes,* I thought and barely nodded my head to give her the nudge I thought she was looking for. How could she not know it was true? Couldn't she feel it? It all made sense. I replayed everything the elders had taught. Didn't it? She turned her gaze back to the missionaries and nodded, slowly, while the rest of her family agreed out loud.

Now all we needed was the cherry cobbler and a scoop of vanilla ice cream.

CHAPTER 19

I HADN'T SEEN MADDI OR HADLEY all day at school, but I'd been thinking about them almost nonstop. There was something new between us, and I wasn't sure how it would change things. The Benson family had agreed to find out the truth. That felt like a big deal—and it felt like I now had an important responsibility to help. Should I be more serious? Should I bear my testimony at lunch? I found myself paying a lot closer attention in seminary during third hour.

So far in life, I felt like I'd learned by osmosis—spiritual info had passively flowed through me because I was in the right place at the right time. I wasn't sure how much I'd actually absorbed, though. Any minute, Maddi or one of the other Bensons might ask me a question with eternal consequences and I was afraid I'd stare blankly, having no idea what the answer was.

I'd been so distracted by thinking about the whole thing during English that I almost missed the reminder about the book report due at the end of the week. It was the last book report of the year and I needed a good grade on it—but didn't even have a book selected yet. Maddi was a library aid the last hour of school, so as soon as the bell rang, I bolted from my classroom and weaved through kids going the opposite direction. I thought maybe she could help me. When I reached for the handle on the double library doors, Hadley emerged from behind me and stepped in front of me, blocking my way.

"Jaxon-Jaxon Quayle," he said. Of course I shook his outstretched hand. "Nice to see you, uh-huh. Lunch was delicious, excellent, accompanied by garlic bread sticks and Italian marinara dipping sauce."

"Yeah, I smelled it cooking all morning. I was going to try to hook up with you guys, but I already had plans to go to lunch with Bucky and a few of the other guys," I said. He didn't shake his head or ask what *I* had for lunch or explain why he'd said anything about lunch at all. He just gave enough time for a random thought to enter my head. It hadn't even occurred to me until that minute that I could've invited him to go to lunch with us. Another time.

"Should we go in?" I asked, since he was still shaking my hand and giving no indication he was going to move any time soon.

"Absolutely." Hadley stepped wide to the right as if part of some practiced routine. I half expected him to salute. "Madelyn Kaye Benson. At the library directly after the final bell rings, uh-huh. Meet immediately in the library."

"You're meeting Maddi here?" I held the door open for both of us to pass through—Hadley first.

"Two-fifty-five p.m. on the dot," he said.

Stepping into the library, I looked at my watch. Three o'clock. "You're late."

"Five whole minutes," Maddi said, coming around the book-filled shelf nearest me and Hadley. She looked great. "I'll let it slide this time," she continued with a grin. "I have a few things I need to finish up, Hadley. Do you think you could find a book to read for a few minutes? Or I think one of the computers is available. I shouldn't be too much longer."

We watched Hadley skim his fingers along a shelved row of books, ultimately making his way to the bank of computers along the back wall.

"Hey," I said.

"Hey yourself."

I could've stood right there for the rest of the afternoon and been happy.

"Technically I'm off duty, but can I help you with something?" she asked, presenting the room with a wave of her hand. "Or have you been holding out on me and you secretly come to the library after school for fun?"

"No," I said. "I came to say hello, and my book report is due Friday. Any ideas?"

She squinted her eyes in concentration. "Hmm, let me think. How about the sequel to *The Scarlet Letter*," she said brightly. "It's right over here." She moved toward a shelf attached to the back wall.

"There's a sequel?" There was no use trying to hide my disappointment. Maddi smiled as if she was about to announce the final answer on "Millionaire" and win all the money.

"Nope."

I stopped.

"Funny."

"It was. You should've seen your face." She continued on to the bookshelf, and I followed as if she had me on a collar and leash. "Does the book have to be about anything in particular?" she asked.

I looked at what I'd written on my hand. "Historical fiction."

"Oh." She did an about-face and her shoulder brushed against my arm as she passed. "Over here," she said.

Reaching the section she was apparently looking for, Maddi pulled out several books halfway, one at a time; each time she seemed to size me up next to the book, and she ended up replacing every one. At one point she pulled out a thick, red book with somebody's picture on the cover; she shook her head and put it back between two others. I yanked it back off the shelf.

"What's wrong with this one?" I asked.

"It's . . . long," she said.

I opened the book to the last page: 623. I shrugged one shoulder as if reading more than six hundred pages in four days was nothing. She cocked her head just like Hadley did, but with one eyebrow up and none of his aloofness. She and I both knew I wouldn't finish it by Friday—or ever. I slid it back on the shelf, trying to look as cool. She chuckled.

"Well, what are you reading right now?" I asked.

"*The Grapes of Wrath* . . ."

"Show-off," I murmured.

She grinned and then added, ". . . and the Book of Mormon."

I nodded my head. Should I say something? Way to go? High-five?

She twisted the ring on her finger and looked at her shoes. "Can I ask you a question?"

Here it comes, I thought. I planted my feet firmly on the industrial carpet as if it would make me think better. "Sure," I said, trying to sound casual.

"Did you know the Book of Mormon has some of the Bible in it?"

That was it? That was the hard question I'd been worrying about?

"Yeah. You mean Isaiah in 2 Nephi, right?" I remembered talking about it in seminary earlier in the year. "I didn't really get it at all until my teacher taught about the symbols and stuff. It's pretty cool."

She nodded. Her face became tense, and she looked toward Hadley, who was greeting people who had come for tutoring, going from table to table with his hand outstretched. I had a sense the question-and-answer period wasn't quite over. She searched my face, seemingly trying to decide whether or not to continue, and then said, "In Alma 11 . . ."

"I thought we were talking about Isaiah."

"Kind of. In 2 Nephi, it talks about the Resurrection and judgment for all of us, so I looked up some other references."

She was taking this seriously—looking up references?

"And," she continued. "In Alma 11, I read that after we die we're resurrected."

"Doesn't your church teach that too?"

"Well, yes, but it's not the same exactly. We believe we'll live again but I never even imagined we could be kind of like we are here—you know, as families, with the same bodies, only, according to what I read, better. I was hoping for heaven . . . angels maybe. I think Alma says something about the body being *made perfect,* restored to *its perfect form.*"

". . . Not so much as a hair of their heads will be lost," I quoted. "I know that one by heart. We've teased my dad about it enough."

Maddi smiled, but it was clear she was still uneasy.

"What's wrong?" I asked.

She twisted her ring again.

"I mean, what if it's true?" I asked. "I'm not trying to be rude, but doesn't that sound better than hanging out in the clouds playing a harp all day?"

She gave me a dirty look that was also half a grin—like for the first time it *did* sound kind of silly to her, but also that I *was* being a little rude.

"Well, doesn't it?" I prodded shamelessly.

"It's not that," she said shaking her head.

I was going to press, but before I could say anything else to get myself in trouble, somebody at a table a few feet behind us broke the "quiet in the library" rule and shouted. "Hadley, really! I'm trying to study!"

Maddi and I turned at the same time to see Hadley leaning uncomfortably far over some kid's shoulder, poking his finger at a page in his textbook. From the way the kid was sitting, fingers laced through his hair and holding his head, it was clear he was struggling with whatever he was working on.

"Two times two, uh-huh, two times two," Hadley said.

Maddi walked calmly toward the table while I watched, standing in front of the historical fiction bookshelf.

"Hadley, what's up? He's studying."

He cocked his head but kept his eyes locked on the book on the table.

"My good friend Michael-Michael Worthen—" Hadley darted his sneak peek toward the kid still holding his head—"needs two times two, uh-huh, two times two for the problem. Two times two." Hadley repeated the equation over and over like he was stuck in a grade-school mantra.

"I *wish* it was that easy!" Hadley's good friend Michael-Michael Worthen said.

"Hey," Maddi said, gently pulling Hadley's arm to make space between him and the kid's chair. "How about I take a look and you go and get my backpack? It's on the floor by Mr. Armstrong's office. I still have some of Mom's cookies in there."

Hadley stood taller.

"Mother Benson's Best Chocolate-Chocolate Chip Toffee," Hadley said, almost as if rehearsing a commercial. "The finest, uh-huh, the very best."

Maddi pointed to Mr. Armstrong's office.

"I think I still have two," she said. "They're all yours if you'll go get it."

Hadley still didn't move.

"Please?" Maddi begged. "I'm almost finished and then we can go."

Hadley tipped his head and slowly slid one foot forward, then the other. Still, he couldn't seem to pry his gaze from the notebook on the table.

"Don't worry. I'll help him," Maddi said. "And then when you get back we can go."

Finally he stepped faster, but barely.

"Sorry," she said to a somewhat calmer Michael Worthen after Hadley was on his way.

Maddi turned back to me and said, "That's what I'm talking about."

Two times two? Michael Worthen? I shook my head, having no idea what she meant.

"The scripture. *Now this restoration shall come to all . . .*" she stated, and her eyes met mine. "What about Hadley?"

"Well, yeah," I said. The thought of what that might mean started to creep into my brain. "Of course Hadley. How cool will that be? Hadley all—"

"Hadley all what?" she asked. "Just like everybody else? Normal?"

I didn't get it. She almost sounded mad.

"Don't you want that?" I asked.

She shook her head, looking at some unseen image.

"I don't know," she said. "I'm not even sure about all of this. *Together forever?* What does that even mean?" And then she leaned closer, her eyes intense and her voice serious. "Am I even going to know him? What if it's not the same between us?" She didn't seem to be asking in a rhetorical way. "What's wrong with him the way he is?"

She waited for an answer. I thought back to the night of prom, when we'd had a similar conversation. The stakes seemed higher now, and I couldn't think of what to say or how to say it.

Hadley bought me some time when he returned with the backpack and aimlessly dropped it on the floor.

"On the bridge, uh-huh, on the bridge times two." He started up right where he'd left off.

At least he wasn't leaning over Michael's shoulder. Instead he was practically laying across the opposite side of the table in order to see the book and point at the problem. Michael Worthen's jaw was clenched and his eyes were closed.

I looked at Maddi and raised both eyebrows. Did I really need to *say* anything?

Maddi lifted her eyes to the ceiling like she might be praying. I'm not sure if it was because of me or Hadley but she once again stepped toward the table, took Hadley by the arm, and tried to tug him away, all the while trying to convince him he wasn't being helpful.

"Madelyn Kaye Benson," Hadley stated, refusing to budge from the table. "I am assisting my friend Michael-Michael Worthen."

He was only Hadley's *friend* Michael-Michael Worthen—not his *good* friend? He must've been ticked.

"Adjacent, adjacent surface bridge components times two," Hadley continued. "The answer is obvious; absolutely plain and clear."

"Okay," Maddi said, her voice strained but controlled, her cheeks darkening. I thought she might take hold of his ankle and pull. "But have you ever thought that Michael-Michael Worthen might not *want* your help?"

Wow. They were arguing. *Michael-Michael Worthen?* She was almost mocking him.

"Let's just go," she said. "But first, why don't you apologize."

Hadley didn't seem to think that was necessary. Instead, he suddenly stood up, resolutely stepped away from Maddi, and continued his *two times two* more and more loudly, rocking at his waist.

I should've helped. I would have, but I'd learned my lesson about not touching him when he was upset—and if he wouldn't listen to Maddi, why would he listen to me?

Mr. Armstrong suddenly came out of his office and was striding toward us quickly, his jaw set.

"Is there a problem here?"

If he only knew.

"No, sir," Maddi said. "Everything's fine." I think she might have said it with the least bit of sarcasm. "Hadley and I were about to leave, as soon as he apologizes. Right, Hadley?"

There we all stood, staring at Hadley, waiting to see what his next move would be. I stepped beside Maddi and leaned close to her ear.

"Absolutely sure you don't want *anything* to change?"

She whipped her head around and the sting of her glare worked as well as if she'd pushed me back with the palm of her hand.

Michael seemed to be the only person in the whole library not leering at our little group. Instead, he leaned closer to his book on the table.

"Wait, wait, wait," he said, "Quiet!"

Amazingly, Hadley stopped chanting. Michael glanced quickly from his notebook to the text and back again.

"*Times two.* I get it! *Both* sides expanding. Coefficient of expansion! Each *adjacent* component expands—*times two.* Man, he's right. Hadley, awesome. Thanks!"

And then he started scribbling, nodding his head with his new-found answer, ignoring everybody else in the room.

With that, Hadley darted a quick glance at Maddi, turned like a cadet, and headed for the library door.

"We're not finished," Maddi said to me, stressing *finished* with a quick poke to my chest. She marched after Hadley.

"Can't wait," I said. *Great.* And I still didn't have a book for my report.

CHAPTER 20

FOR THE REST OF THE WEEK, we still said hello if we passed each other in the hall. Hadley, Maddi, and I even ate lunch together in the cafeteria a couple of times—Hadley insisted, sitting in the middle—but it was tense. And something always got in the way of continuing the conversation Maddi and I had started in the library. I really didn't know what I'd say if we talked about it, but I didn't like the obvious strain between us.

Then the Bensons came to church the next Sunday. There was a missionary farewell and although we were early, the chapel was filling up. Once the Jeppsens realized the Bensons were investigators, they happily gave up their regular seats—even when it meant sitting in some of the metal chairs lined up in the cultural hall. My family and the Bensons mingled together across the last two benches in the chapel.

Hadley was already a kind of celebrity in our ward. Some of the youth knew him from school and most of the guys still thought of him as a golf pro—a different kind of golf pro, maybe, but still a hero.

Several of the adults remembered Hadley from his first visit and said how much his musical number had meant to them. Was he going to play for them again?

"Perhaps another time would be appropriate," he said. "Another Sabbath would be most acceptable, uh-huh, lovely. Today, however, I am here to listen and observe."

I probably could've made some extra money if I'd had autographed pictures of him.

After the elders arrived and sat next to "Brother and Sister" Benson, my brother Jarom and I went to the front to pass and bless the sacrament.

"Cool," Bucky said when I sat next to him on the bench, referring to the Bensons with a nod of his head. I grinned. It was nice having them at church for the first time.

Hadley insisted that he sit on the last row in the seat closest to the aisle, Maddi next, then two of her little sisters next to my sister Kristin, and then my brothers Brady and Alex. Everybody else sat on the bench in front of them. I could watch their faces from where I sat and wondered what the Bensons were thinking. I'd never been to a meeting of another religion. I thought it'd probably be weird.

Since the missionaries had arrived just before the meeting started, I doubted they'd had much time to explain how things went. Maybe the Bensons were waiting for a preacher to stand up in front and shout from the pulpit with everybody answering *amen* after each sentence. I'd seen something like that on television. I didn't know what they were expecting, but when it came time for me to say the sacrament prayer, my hands were cold and I was saying a simultaneous prayer that my voice wouldn't crack. I opened my eyes and stood to hand the trays to the other guys. All the Bensons were watching me. I knew my face was red.

When the tray reached the first Quayle-Benson row, my shoulders tensed. Had anybody told the Bensons what they were supposed to do? They had to know something about the sacrament, since they all seemed to understand the Bible so well. Still, I wasn't sure how it worked in their church, and I wondered if they'd take the bread or pass the tray along without partaking. Mr. Benson declined; a ripple of taps and glances with a subtle shaking of heads between the Bensons moved down both rows. Only members of my family took pieces of bread. No problem, until the tray reached the end of the row where Hadley sat.

Heel clicks echoed in the cultural hall as Tanner and Rachel walked in, arm in arm, laughing in a loud whisper as if they didn't realize they were disrupting the sacrament. I should've known he'd come. Clint, the missionary who was going to speak, was on Tanner's baseball team before Clint graduated. Hadley wasn't the only one who turned to see what the commotion was, but when he twisted in his seat, he knocked the tray with his elbow, sending the remaining pieces of bread airborne.

I gasped. Bucky held my arm just above the elbow when I tried to jump from my seat. "They've got it," he whispered. The deacon next to Hadley crouched down immediately and began gathering bread from the aisle floor. The little girls sitting next to Hadley plucked pieces from the bench and wherever else they'd landed.

Probably to make sure anybody that hadn't noticed would, Tanner snickered out loud and pointed at Hadley. Maddi glanced at Tanner. When she turned forward again, her eyes were squinted and her lips made a thin line.

"What's his problem?" I asked, probably too loudly, with heat rising up my neck.

"He's an idiot," Bucky whispered right back. There were no big vocabulary words this time.

Most of the people sitting around Hadley and Maddi gave understanding smiles. Even though I noticed color creeping up Maddi's neck and into her cheeks as the others put the gathered bread into the tray she still held, I relaxed.

Tanner must have realized he wasn't getting the reaction he looked for and finally sat down next to Rachel. When I tried to burn the obnoxious smirk off of his face with my glare, he looked straight at me and held his hands out with a *what?*

Way to make a great first church-going impression, Tanner.

Through all the commotion, Hadley sat as if nothing had happened except for a slight rocking motion, which he sometimes did anyway. I almost wished he'd walk straight back to Tanner and punch him. Instead he watched the last piece of bread land in the tray while Maddi calmly handed it back to the deacon with a soft smile. Then she lifted her eyes to mine.

"Sorry," she mouthed, as if she had anything to apologize for. I held Maddi's gaze and shrugged back with a grin, hopefully letting her know it was okay.

As badly as I wanted to sit by Maddi after the bishop had excused us to sit with our families, I didn't want to cause another scene by disturbing Hadley's seating chart. I sat on the bench in front of them and used all of my self-control to keep from turning my head every five seconds to look back at her. Thankfully, the first couple of talks were pretty good. One of the girls in my Sunday School class gave a talk on how Personal Progress helped her testimony grow, and Clint spoke about faith. Both seemed like good topics for people just learning about the Church, and the whole sacrament-passing incident started to fade in my mind. I actually paid attention to the speakers when I wasn't wondering what the Benson family was thinking—especially Maddi. Maybe I was being selfish in a way, but I wanted her more than any of the others to feel it.

I got a little worried when Brother Belkin from the high council stood to speak. There were more than twenty minutes left, and nearly every high councilman had a reputation for being long and dry. Brother Belkin was no exception.

"Have you ever wondered where you came from?" he began. "Why you're here and where you're going?"

Normally, this would have been my nap trigger. How many times had I heard those questions before? But suddenly they became really important, especially the first one. Sacrament meeting couldn't end soon enough. I had to talk to Maddi. I knew how to answer her questions about Hadley.

CHAPTER 21

"You knew him before," I said.

Maddi and I sat beside each other, legs outstretched, on the grass under a big, leafy tree outside the meetinghouse. The weather was perfect, and people were streaming from the double doors and moving to their cars. After the meeting, Tanner was too busy basking in Clint's glory to bother picking on anybody.

Several people rushed the Benson family after the final amen, welcoming them and saying how happy they were about them visiting. Considering the mass of new people, I think Maddi was more willing to slip out when I asked if I could talk to her. Hadley didn't even try to come with us. Church seemed to be his own kind of heaven where hand-shaking was practically doctrinal.

"Knew who before? When?" Maddi asked, confused.

"Hadley. Before you came to earth."

Her expression didn't show any more clarity about what I'd said.

"Remember the other day in the library?" I asked. Only one of her eyebrows lifted. "I know. I plan on apologizing in a minute, but first, you said you were afraid that if Hadley was different when he was resurrected, you might not know him, at least not in the same way."

Maddi's face relaxed except for a questioning crease between her eyes as she nodded slowly.

"You knew him before," I repeated. "Before you came to earth, in the pre-existence. I thought about how you came together as twins. You were probably really close there. There's no way you won't know him."

"The pre-*existence*," she said, sounding just as skeptical as if I'd asked her to go on a trip to the moon, but then something seemed to click. "Wait—the last talk in church. That man said something about it, right?"

"Yeah," I said. "That's what made me think of it."

Maddi shook her head. "I've gone to church my whole life and nobody has ever said anything about that. It sounds weird."

Weird was not the response I had hoped for.

"You believe in heaven, right?" I asked. "Going there after we die?"

"Yeah," she agreed reluctantly, as if waiting for a trap to spring. "At least I hope I'll go there."

I could only smirk at her comment. If she didn't make it, I was a lost cause for sure.

"Anyway," I said dramatically, rolling my eyes and then continuing, "if you believe in a life *after* we die, why is it such a leap to believe in a life before we were born?"

"Before we were born?" The crease between her eyes deepened. "I've never even thought about that before," she said.

"Really?" The concept felt part of me. It was just something I knew, like the Word of Wisdom. It was a no-brainer.

"God created us and then we were born," she said as if reciting from a handbook. "You're saying we all lived together before? Me? You? Everybody?" She seemed to search my face for answers. The intensity in her voice begged me to explain further. Suddenly there was pressure. I didn't think this would be that big of a deal. I'd point out the obvious, she'd realize it made perfect sense, and then she'd hug me with a tear in her eye in thanks for the brilliant insight. Quick and easy. I looked away, fidgeting, trying to appear as if I was searching for a simple way to explain all of my profound wisdom instead of stalling for time, wishing I'd waited to bring this up until the missionaries were there to bail me out.

"Yeah," I finally said. "Everybody."

The Bensons' car pulled against the curb not too far from where we sat before she could ask more questions. *Great save,* I thought with relief. I rolled to my knees, stood, and held out a hand to help Maddi up.

"Ready to go?" her dad called through the open window.

Hadley, who was sitting in the backseat, rolled down his own window and stuck out his hand. With all the shaking he did, I wondered if one day his arm would be permanently angled.

"Jaxon-Jaxon Quayle," Hadley said in his all-too-familiar way.

We walked to the car. Maddi went to her dad's window and I went to Hadley's, reaching out to grip his hand.

"Hey, Hadley," I said. "How was church?"

"Excellent. Uh-huh. Excellent and informative. Members of the Burley Seventh Ward were both exceptional and inviting. I plan to visit again next week."

I chuckled at his answer. "I hope you do," I said. "I'm sure everybody would like to get to know you better."

I was about to tell Maddi we could finish talking later when she surprised me and asked permission to walk home with me. There was an unspoken agreement between her parents marked by a nodding of heads.

"Don't be too long," Mr. Benson said as he put the car in drive and began to pull away slowly. Hadley still had hold of my hand.

"Let go, Hadley," Maddi said calmly. "Dad's leaving."

I only had to jog a few steps before he released his grip. Mr. Benson's sharp "Hadley!" probably helped.

Maddi and I walked beside each other, the sun warming my back. This afternoon would've been perfect except for the looming discussion. Maddi obviously wanted to start right where we had left off.

"Okay, so your church really believes we lived in heaven before we were born?" Maddi asked as we watched her family disappear around the corner. "Why?"

I scrambled through all the Primary, Sunday School, and other church lessons I could remember. I knew this stuff. I pictured the visual aids. Everybody was in white, smiling and happy. I did. I *knew* this stuff.

"To learn, I guess. To choose whether we wanted to come to Earth. To decide who we'd follow."

"Follow?" she asked.

"Jesus or Satan." And then I found myself reciting everything I knew about the plan of salvation while we strolled down the sidewalk. Maddi listened intently, interrupting only a couple of times to ask questions.

"Wow," she said when I finished. "That's a lot to take in."

"But do you see what I mean now?" I asked. "If you and Hadley knew each other before—before he got a body—plus all the time you'll spend together here, then you'll know each other even better after you're resurrected."

"*If* we were there before," she said.

"You were," I said with more conviction than I expected, an idea starting to form. "Why do you love Hadley so much?"

Maddi's eyes registered something like surprise. "He's my brother," she answered.

"Yeah, but you don't treat him like I treat my brothers," I said.

"Maybe you should work on that," she countered.

"Probably," I agreed with a half smile. "But think about it. More than anything, you should resent him. Look at all the extra attention he gets and all the time you've had to spend with him right from the start. You have a right to be mad about it, but you're not. Why do you think that is?"

She seemed unable to answer, staring down as if she couldn't quite figure out where to look on the page. "We're twins," she finally said. "Maybe it's because we've always been together."

"Right. I think you *have* always been together, and not just here. Your mom's known him his whole life too, and Hadley lets you do things for him he doesn't let her. Do you really think it's only because you shared some space for nine months?"

She hesitated. "Other twins are close," she said, frustration creeping into her voice. "You wouldn't understand. I just *get* him and I know it doesn't always seem like it, but he understands me too."

"That's exactly my point. I like Hadley, especially the longer I know him, but I think you see something more in him than the rest of us."

Maddi didn't respond.

"Okay," I continued. "Let's just say there was a pre-existence and you were there with your whole family. You didn't have bodies yet, not like you do now. You were all just spirits, as perfect as you could be, but then you learned about how life would be here—kind of like a preview. I think you and Hadley were already close, but then you found out his life was going to be, I don't know, more challenging."

I thought about how people scooted back a step when Hadley wanted to shake their hands because he stood just a little too close. I thought about the way they spoke to him in an almost childish voice, more slowly, choosing their words too carefully. I pictured the way his shirt was always tucked in, the perfect part in his hair, the way he rocked at his waist when things bugged him, and the tight way people smiled at him.

Sometimes Maddi had to convince Hadley to do things he didn't want to do; maybe sometimes he embarrassed her, but I could hear her calm voice in my head. She never talked down to him, even when she was frustrated—like the other day in the library—and I thought about the way Hadley *allowed* her to help him when nobody else could.

"Maybe the two of you had a plan. I think you promised to help each other get through life the best way you could. That seems like something you'd do. You care about everybody, way more than I do, but even with that, there's something different about the two of you. I'm not sure how to say it. I guess it's that Hadley lets you, and only you, in a place nobody else can go."

I couldn't read what Maddi was thinking, but when we walked onto her front lawn, she reached for my hand and held it, just for a second, and then let it go. She moved toward her door but I stepped in front of her to block her way.

"Wait. Don't you think there's a *possibility* you knew each other before?" I asked. "That you came here together for a reason? That maybe Hadley needed you?"

Maddi lifted her chin.

"No," she said defiantly. "We needed each other."

CHAPTER 22

THE LAST MONTH OF SCHOOL was crazy. I went to class, studied, and played soccer. That was about it. Our team made it to playoffs but lost in the semifinal rounds. I wasn't happy about it, but knew I had two more years to play. We'd get there. I did go to a few of the girls' softball games; Maddi had made the team and played second base. Hadley was always her biggest fan, and just like at our informal soccer game earlier in the year, he started each game by shouting, "PLAY BALL!"

Hadley seemed to have made himself an honorary umpire, and he wore a bright orange t-shirt with big, black letters that read: *Whether I'm right or wrong, I'm right!* From the looks the *real* umpire gave him, I don't think he always appreciated Hadley's calls. Still, it seemed like most of the crowd couldn't help getting caught up in his enthusiasm, and almost everybody ended up looking like ridiculously supportive fans—me included.

Honestly, Maddi was better at soccer, but she was pretty good at softball too—she threw hard and fast and hit as well as most of the girls on the team. She'd even made a home run a couple of weeks earlier when the other team's fielder dropped the ball. I loved the look on her face when she made the slide. It was intense. We all went for ice cream that day, but other than that, we hadn't spent much time together.

I'd been going pretty hard, so I was really ready for the last week of school. Finals were over, sports were finished for the season, and all I had to do was show up, go to a few assemblies, and sign yearbooks.

I'd been looking for Bucky—and Maddi, really—since after first hour, the only required class on the last day of school, but hadn't found either one of them. They were giving yearbooks out in the gym, so I went there. Tables had been set up and volunteers were handing out yearbooks alphabetically.

There were so many kids waiting that I couldn't see the signs that indicated which line I needed to stand in. I picked one near the left side of the gym and hoped it was right. It moved quickly, and before long I was near the front of the line.

I *heard* Hadley before I saw him.

"Madelyn Kaye Benson," he said loudly. "There is entirely too much confusion. Another time would be better. Uh-huh, perhaps yearbooks would be better received through the mail."

When I turned to look, I noticed Hadley was rocking too rapidly and Maddi had her *calm-Hadley-down* face on. I wasn't sure what to do. There were only three people in front of me.

I couldn't hear what Maddi was saying over the noise of the crowd, but I recognized the growing agitation in Hadley and saw the color moving into Maddi's cheeks.

"No-no-no!" He shouted. "Absolutely not. We will call mother immediately, uh-huh, call her now and she will come at once!"

Hadley would have attracted less attention if he was dressed like a clown and doing the hula.

I grabbed a book from the short stack on the table in front of me—my mom had pre-paid—and hurried to where Maddi and Hadley stood near the entrance of the gym.

"Hadley, I've been waiting for you," I said on a hunch. "I want you to be the first one to sign my yearbook. You can write on any page you choose."

His rocking slowed and he gave me what I'd started to call his sneak peek.

"I have three pens you can choose from," I coaxed, smiling as if Hadley wasn't on the verge of a meltdown. I pulled the markers from my back pocket and held them up.

Maddi bit her bottom lip, but when Hadley took noticeable interest in the yearbook and then slowly reached for the silver pen, she started to grin.

We followed Hadley over to the lowest bench on the set of bleachers and waited for him to get seated. He lifted the cover of my yearbook and then started the process of searching for exactly the right place to sign, turning page after page.

"Do you and Hadley have your yearbooks yet?" I asked Maddi once Hadley seemed engrossed.

She shook her head.

"I've got this. Go ahead and get in line."

"Are you sure?" she asked, like I was crazy to risk being alone with him.

"It's not like you won't know if I do something to set him off again," I said. "It's fine."

She hesitated, but then Maddi went to find the right line, A–E, and I sat next to Hadley and waited. Before he finished with mine, two more kids asked if he'd sign theirs too. His whole mood seemed to change.

Of course he was "delighted, uh-huh, happy too."

Bucky and Heather found us at about the same time Maddi came back carrying two yearbooks.

"High-five," Bucky said without actually high-fiving anybody. "Right on time for the yearbook shuffle." And then we started swapping books until we each held one belonging to somebody else in our loose circle.

Bucky plopped right onto the floor, leaning against the lowest bench of the bleacher and started writing. Heather sat next to him, but on the bench, and Maddi and I sat on either side of Hadley. Everything was cool as the books went around until Maddi's open book rested in my lap. Suddenly there was pressure. What should I write? *Have a fun summer. Call me?* Or did I use a whole page and write what I really wanted to say? I stared blankly until Maddi gently slid my book beneath hers. *That was fast.* I turned my body away, hoping to stop her from noticing as I looked for what she'd written. I glanced to see her already signing another book and then thumbed through pages until I found it. Under the picture of Hadley's class—Mrs. Holmes, room 32—she'd written in perfect handwriting.

Thanks . . . for everything.

Love,

Maddi

And then I knew what to write and I found the same picture in her book.

Any time.

CHAPTER 23

THE SUN HAD ONLY BEEN up for a couple of hours when Bucky and I knocked on the Bensons' door, but it was already warm. I sucked in a deep breath. Their family had just returned from a reunion in Nebraska and I was curious about whether they might have regrets about moving away now that they'd gone back. Maybe I'd get a chance to find out during fireworks.

Since school had been out, I'd spent a week at Scout camp, another week at soccer camp, and a few days backpacking with my family, so I'd barely seen the Bensons.

For some sissy reason, I was tense.

"What're you worried about?" Bucky said. "She's probably going to swoon all over herself when she sees you."

"Swoon? Who says that?"

He only grinned.

We heard pounding feet and lots of laughing. It sounded like the whole family was racing to be the first to answer the door. Chloe, the youngest, won, but still had a hard time opening the door all the way with the kids trying to stick their heads out to see who was standing on the front porch.

"Hey, girls," I said. "Is Hadley here?"

"It's just Jaxon and his friend," Chloe said, but nobody moved until I heard Maddi.

"Okay, guys. It's for Hadley. Let him through," she said. "Chloe, let go of the doorknob."

And just like that, the sea of Benson kids parted. Maddi and Hadley stepped to the threshold.

I almost covered my chest with my hand, afraid everybody could see my heart pounding. Instead I beat Hadley to it and held it out for him to shake.

"Ready to go?" I asked, talking to Hadley, but stealing glances at Maddi.

Bucky and I were taking Hadley with us to the park to find a place for all of our families to sit together during fireworks that night.

"Absolutely—absolutely ready to stake out our spot at Burley Golf Course by the river in Burley, Idaho," Hadley said. "But no golf today, uh-huh, no golf, just picnics, fireworks, and loud music for the Fourth of July."

"That about sums it up," I said.

He cocked his head and then stepped between me and Bucky. Bucky jumped from the porch and bolted toward the car.

"First one there gets shotgun," he shouted over his shoulder to Hadley; then he slowed to a jog, letting Hadley catch up. Maddi was still grinning when I turned toward her.

"Sure you don't want to come?" I said, taking a half step forward.

"And mess with the macho bonding going on?" She pretended like she was shocked I'd even asked. "No way. I have a *lot* of picnic preparation," she said solemnly. "Very important responsibility—fried chicken, brownies, and the most delicious potato salad in all the universe."

"Sorry," I said looking at my feet sadly. "But I'm pretty sure there's no such thing as delicious potato salad."

"*Obviously*, you have not had *my* potato salad," she said, shoving me backward with her palm against my chest. I grabbed her wrist to keep from falling off the porch. I don't know what happened, but I didn't let go, even after I had my balance. I just slid my hand down hers until our fingers linked up. We looked at our hands together and then I slowly lifted my eyes to her face. She didn't let go.

It was ridiculously like the movies. There might have been music playing. Time froze. I so wanted to lean in and kiss her but Hadley laid on the horn and we both jumped like we'd touched an electric fence with wet hands. The music in my head screeched to a stop and we laughed nervously.

"I guess he's ready," I said pointing to the car.

"Yeah, he can be a little impatient sometimes."

I could've stayed on the porch with her all day, but I slowly let go of her hand and turned to leave when he honked again.

"See ya later," I said.

"See ya. And, hey," she called as I grabbed the door handle, "take care of my brother. No losing him on the golf course again," she teased.

"I'll do my best," I said. "As long as he doesn't turn into a show-off."

I drove with Hadley in the passenger seat and Bucky in the middle of the back. When we got to the mostly empty course—closed for the Fourth, except for the driving range—there were already a few chairs roped together on the lawn and some people had laid out quilts out. There were still good spots, and we'd have a perfect view of the fireworks over the river.

Tanner and Shawn showed up right after we did. They barely glanced at us while spreading three blankets and setting a few chairs not too far from where we were. I hoped they were leaving when they went back to their car, but they came back holding something between them. They guarded whatever it was as if they were carrying plans for some top-secret mission. I probably should've paid better attention when they crouched in front of the bushes that ran in a row not too far from the blankets we were spreading and turned their backs to us, but I didn't want them to think I cared. They apparently thought they were pretty funny by the way they kept laughing.

Between the Bensons, Bucky's family, and my family, we had a lot of lawn to cover with old quilts. Hadley stayed busy picking off any grass that flipped onto the quilts as we spread them out. It must've been really important to gather every single blade, because he kept at it, making a straight, careful pile in his hand, even after we reminded him they'd get dirty again when people walked on them.

"Hadley," I said after we'd finally smoothed the last one. "Want to help us find some rocks to hold the blankets down in case the wind blows while we're gone?"

The wind blew in Burley almost every day, at least for a while.

"Possibly," he said. "Possibly, but there are still many pieces of grass, many pieces to collect from the blankets."

"Okay. Well, when you're finished, you can come and help. We'll be down by the river." I felt safer being between him and the water, and Bucky and I could take turns making sure he stayed where we could see him.

We carried only two or three rocks at a time, since they had to be big enough to hold the blankets in place if the wind blew very hard. We'd gather a few just off the bank where the rocks were bigger, and then we'd walk back and place them on the edges of the quilts. I'd been doing this same thing for years, but it still didn't occur to me to bring a wheelbarrow. And even though I ran almost every morning and was in decent shape, I breathed hard by the third or fourth turn. Bucky was moving more slowly too.

"Want to take a turn getting rocks?" I asked Hadley after setting mine down on the corners. I sat on the grass beside him, mostly to catch a quick rest. I was careful not to kick any grass onto the blanket.

"No thank you, Jaxon Quayle," he said. "It is very important for the quilts to remain tidy for the picnic—very important."

"I'm sure there can't be too much more grass on them," I said. "You've been working at it for a long time. Besides, if we get done soon we might be able to get ice cream."

He hesitated.

"Ice cream—pralines and cream, my one and only favorite. Good idea. Very good idea." He picked only one more piece of grass from an ugly floral blanket and then stood awkwardly and cocked his head, almost looking at me from the corner of his eye. Bucky held up his hand to high-five Hadley and then jogged ahead.

"Last one there's a moldy carp!" he shouted back at us.

"You are cheating, Bucky Jay Wilkinson—cheating by starting the race before all the runners are set."

"Come on!" I yelled and then sprinted toward Bucky. I caught up to him easily but then he turned up the speed. I ran faster and then he ran faster, and soon we went full bore, racing toward the river. We reached the bank at about the same time, laughing and out of breath.

"Hadley," I reminded, bent over and sucking air. I looked over my shoulder to see how far behind he was, but he wasn't anywhere near. I walked up onto the berm. He was trudging away from us, toward the clump of bushes Tanner and Shawn had huddled in front of earlier.

"If you get a few more rocks," I said to Bucky. "I'll run back and find out what he's doing."

I'd barely started to jog in Hadley's direction when Tanner and Shawn jumped up from behind a car in the parking lot. They were waving their arms, shouting and running straight at Hadley. "No! Stop!" They yelled. Hadley paused, glancing their way briefly, but then continued forward. I squinted at the bushes he was moving toward. There was a large brown paper bag on the ground in front of them, the top folded over. I glanced at Tanner and Shawn, who'd slowed their pace and were shouting at each other excitedly. They were either nervous or scared—I could see it on their faces and in the way they moved. Something was wrong, and I immediately felt panic rise up my chest and into my throat. I started running again, harder than I had to the river. I couldn't get to Hadley fast enough.

Pop-pop-pop-pop-pop-pop-pop!

Every boy over twelve knows the sound of a string of firecrackers going off.

Hadley fell backward, covering his ears, rolling back and forth erratically. Then another round of popping burst the air.

"Too loud!" he shouted. "Too loud! Too loud! Too loud!"

And then another eruption. Hadley wailed in confusion, his eyes wide with fear and pain. I could see it in the way he curled into a ball and shook.

"It's okay," I shouted. I'd almost reached him. "It's just noise, Hadley! It's just noise!" But when I finally knelt beside him, I realized it was more than *just noise*. Hadley was splattered—his face, his hair, his clothing—and the smell of dog crap made me want to wretch. I turned on Tanner and Shawn who stood frozen above me and Hadley.

"What did you do?" I screamed. Their faces were pale; neither answered. They stared down at Hadley. "What did you do?" I yelled, anger and fear making the words explode from my mouth. Hadley writhed beside me, moaning like an injured cat.

"Too loud . . . too loud . . . too loud," he whimpered, one hand covering his ear and the other trying to rid himself of the dog mess.

"We didn't think . . ." Tanner stammered.

"No kidding," I said through clenched teeth.

"It was just supposed to get the blankets," he said.

"Yeah, well . . ." I really didn't want to hear anything he had to say.

"What's going on?" Bucky asked, jogging toward us.

I didn't see Bucky because I was focused on Hadley, but Bucky must've caught on pretty quickly. "What the—" He kneeled beside Hadley, opposite me. "Hey buddy, you okay?" Hadley didn't respond to him any better than he had to me.

I pulled off my shirt, leaning in to wipe Hadley's face. I'd barely brushed it when he jerked away as if my touch had burned him like acid; he yelled as if he was terrified. He swung his arms wildly, hitting me against the side of my head with all his adrenaline-powered strength, knocking me to the ground. Without warning, Hadley scrambled to his feet and bolted toward the river.

"Hadley!" I called, standing unsteadily, blinking back the darkness swimming in and out of sight. "Hadley, wait!" But he didn't seem to hear me. He ran, darting crazily across the green, toward the rocky berm. I turned back and shouted to Bucky, "Get help!" Then I ran after Hadley.

I was a faster runner, but Hadley had a sizable head start and I didn't have great focus after having been hit. I pushed through the fogginess and ran as hard as I could, calling his name over and over, hoping he'd hear me and at least slow down. But he kept going, closer and closer to the river. What then? He'd have to stop, right? I didn't even know if he could swim—didn't even know if it mattered with the state he was in.

"Hadley!" I had to get to him before he reached the water. I didn't have a choice.

He'd stumble over his own feet and the gap between us would almost close, but then he'd dart off to the side, zig-zag away from me, and shoot off across the grass. Every time he evaded me, I felt like somebody had tightened the hinge in my jaw.

"Come on, Hadley. Knock it off!" My throat burned from running. My pulse pounded in my ears, my side ached, and hot irritation swelled in my chest. He'd probably freak even more when I caught him, but if I was ready for him—if I gripped him tightly enough, maybe pinned him to the ground—I might be able to hold him long enough for help to get there. The incline of the embankment finally slowed his pace enough for me to get a piece of his sleeve.

He tried to dart away. *Not this time!* I'd had enough.

"Hadley, stop!" Instead of veering away, he leaped for the top of the berm at the same time I lunged, wrapping both of my arms around him tightly. We both went down hard, each losing our footing against the pile of stacked stones. The loud *crack* of his head against rock silenced every other sound but the echo in my head.

CHAPTER 24

WE ROLLED OFF THE EMBANKMENT, toppling over each other two or three times until we finally came to a stop on the dirt at the bottom of the berm. Hadley didn't care if I touched him now. He'd stopped moaning. He wasn't writhing, and his eyes were closed. His mouth gaped open. A stream of blood from the back of his head oozed toward my knees as I knelt beside him once again. My heart pounded and my brain seemed unable to engage until Maddi's voice rang repeatedly in my head.

"Hey, take care of my brother."

What had I done? I placed my hand on Hadley's chest, waiting for the rise and fall of it.

He was breathing. My vision blurred and I roughly wiped at the tears threatening to spill over. Suddenly, his eyes opened.

"Hadley?"

His arm moved into me once, twice, a third time, almost as if he was tapping to get my attention. But there was something wrong. His eyes were empty and his whole body began to quiver until it shook like somebody was bouncing him on a trampoline.

I pulled back. "Hadley!" I shouted this time and then put both hands on his shoulders, trying to help him stop shaking. His eyes rolled back until all I could see was mostly white. Spit foamed around his mouth and drooled down the side.

"Help!" I shouted.

I scrambled around on my knees and did my best to cushion his lurching neck and head. Blood covered my hands and wicked into the hem of my shorts. My shirt gone, I looked for anything to stop the bleeding. There was nothing.

Help him. Please, help him; I repeated in my mind, realizing I hoped Heavenly Father was listening.

Hadley took a desperate, gasping breath and then lay still. Mingled with all of the other odors, I smelled urine.

I lifted my head when I heard a golf cart rolling over the gravel of one of the paths winding through the nearby course. The engine stopped and Bucky came over the hill.

"What can I do?" he asked, standing over us, his face tight with concern.

"He's bleeding," I said. My voice sounded far away, like I wasn't really sure if I'd spoken.

Bucky scrambled down the rocks, holding something like a tackle box marked *First Aid Kit*.

"Yeah. When I saw the two of you go down, I got this from the clubhouse."

Bucky snapped open the case and grabbed a roll of gauze. "Here," he said.

I held the wad against Hadley's wound, but it was saturated in seconds.

"Call 911," I said.

"Already did," he said, and held up his cell phone. "But the police might be at the clubhouse by now anyway. The manager called them about Tanner and Shawn. He's holding them there until the police arrive. Will you guys be okay if I go back and check?"

"Hurry," I said.

Bucky bounded back over the hill and I listened to the sound of the golf cart fade away before I could say anything more. I held Hadley's head in my lap, afraid to move—afraid he might wake up and afraid he might not.

The next few minutes felt like a surreal blur. I heard the return of the cart again but this time Bucky had a police officer with him. He was there just long enough to check Hadley's pulse and ask each of our names when sirens sounded in the distance; the officer seemed as relieved as I was at the sound. Bucky stood at the top of the berm, waving them forward. The same gravel crunched under tires, only louder, and a more powerful engine than just a golf cart drew nearer. Three or four people wearing uniforms and carrying bags swooped down on us like birds. I didn't move. I carefully placed one hand on Hadley's chest and left the other under his head.

"Son, what's your name?" one of the men asked as his partner rushed in to check Hadley's breathing, listen to his heart, look into his eyes.

My body started to tremble.

"Jaxon," I managed to say.

"Okay, Jaxon. You need to let us check him now. Can you help me? I'm going to put this brace under him to steady his head and neck and then you need to slide your hand out carefully. Okay?"

I nodded and did what he asked, even though I doubted a neck brace was going to do anything to help after how hard Hadley had been flopping.

"He was shaking," I said. "All over." My voice sounded relatively calm even though my head buzzed so loudly I barely heard myself.

The man nodded. "We'll take care of him," he said. "Do you think you can stand up now?"

Somehow I stood and then Bucky was there, helping me. The ground seemed to tip and I struggled to keep my balance. Another EMT took me by the elbow on the other side.

"Why don't we go to the truck?" he asked, indicating the back of the ambulance.

"I want to stay," I said. "He'll be scared."

"We'll take care of him."

I stared at Hadley on the ground. He looked like any other kid.

"No, it's not like that. He's—" What? What was he?

"He's sorta . . . different," Bucky explained.

"Yeah, okay. Still, I think you need to sit down. Just for a minute," he continued, leading me to the bumper. I did feel steadier after I sat down—and since we were only a few feet away, I could still see them work on Hadley.

"Jax, I'm supposed to give a report to the police officer. You okay?" Bucky asked while the EMT pulled a dark gray blanket from his bag and draped it around my bare back and shoulders. *Was I?* I didn't know. My teeth chattered in spite of the hot sun. "I'll be right back," he said.

"Yeah . . . Thanks for . . ."

He shrugged *no problem* and walked toward another uniform.

I pulled the blanket tighter and then clasped the edges with one hand. My hand was red and sticky. There was even blood under my fingernails.

"I need to ask you some questions," the EMT said. "You okay with that?"

I must've nodded.

"Good. Do you know if he's on any medication?"

I shook my head. I didn't know.

"His name?"

"Hadley-Hadley Benson," I sounded just like him.

"You related?"

"No, he's my friend." *My friend, my very good friend, Hadley-Hadley Benson.* "Is he going to be okay?" I asked. "He's not waking up."

"He's postictal," the EMT explained. "Sometimes people are really sleepy after a seizure."

A seizure. Of course he'd had a seizure. I'd flat out tackled him. Me. I'd done that. On the rocks. I looked at the darkening red on my hands again. What did I think was going to happen? *So stupid. So, so stupid.*

"Is this . . . feces?" I heard the woman working on Hadley ask. "What happened here?" But by the disgusted look registering on her face, she already knew. She darted a quick, questioning, almost angry glance my way.

"I didn't—"

"Why don't you tell me exactly what happened?" asked the EMT who had been helping me. His voice sounded a little harsher as he seemed to guess what the blood and the splatters covering Hadley might mean.

What did he want me to say? That I could barely think straight? That Tanner and Shawn were jerks? That if I had stayed with Hadley like I should have, if I hadn't made him hit his head, he wouldn't be hurt? I should be taking him to get ice cream—two scoops of pralines and cream—not answering some guy's questions and watching emergency people swarm all over Hadley.

But before I could say anything, Hadley began a steady whimper and pushed weakly at the woman's probing hands. He was so pale.

"I might need some help over here," she said.

"He doesn't like to be touched," I said, as if that mattered now. At least he was moving.

"Wait here," the male EMT ordered. A police officer from the squad car that had pulled in just after the ambulance came striding toward me, a notebook and pen in hand.

"You Jaxon Quayle?" he asked.

I nodded.

"I need to ask you some questions."

More questions. I stared blankly until I noticed Tanner and Shawn in the back seat of the police car. All my fear was suddenly replaced by rage, and I wanted to tear into Tanner. I didn't care that he looked like he was about to throw up. I hoped he was terrified, and I hoped Shawn felt the same way. I told the officer everything, beginning with picking Hadley up at his house until the moment the police had arrived. I tried to explain about Hadley so the officer could understand how much worse Tanner's prank really was—and I made sure I said Tanner's whole name clearly and loudly.

By the time I'd finished, Bucky thrust out his hand to help me up so they could load Hadley into the ambulance.

"I want to ride with him," I said.

"I'm sorry, but you're not family," the EMT said.

"He'll be scared if he wakes up." I looked at my feet. "And I need to explain to his family. Please just let me ride with him."

The EMT paused, glancing from Hadley to me.

"You done with him?" he asked the policeman.

"For now," he said, seeming to think the whole situation over in his head. He looked from Tanner and Shawn in the backseat to Hadley in the ambulance to me. "Let him ride. It's not that far to the hospital. I'll catch him there if I have any more questions."

The EMT shrugged his okay.

"Thanks," I said. I threw Bucky my car keys. "Tell my mom." Bucky pulled his shirt over his head, tossed it to me, and nodded.

Riding in the ambulance wasn't like in the movies. I sat in the passenger seat and hardly saw what was happening with Hadley. He was mostly quiet, but once in a while he whimpered like a little kid having a nightmare—mumbling words you couldn't quite understand, crying just long enough to wonder if we shouldn't try to wake him up. Why didn't he wake up?

The closer we got to the hospital, the stronger the pulse throbbed in my neck. The Bensons would be there—his mom, his dad . . . Maddi. What was I going to say? There was no way to explain, no way to make it okay.

"Could we clean him up some?" I asked. I couldn't let them see him like he was now. I leaned over the armrest to talk to the EMT nearest Hadley. "His family—"

"We're pulling into the hospital now," she said. "They're waiting for him."

"Please. At least his face."

She held my gaze for only a second. "Hold up a minute, Tim," she said, and the ambulance slowed. The woman tore open a package and began gently wiping the mess from Hadley's face. He only moaned as he halfheartedly turned his head away.

"Okay," she said when she'd finished. "That's the best I can do. Let's go."

Hadley's family met the stretcher on the sidewalk outside the emergency room door while I got out and then stood with my back toward the driver's side of the ambulance. The fear and worry in their faces was bad enough, but when it registered just what it was that mottled Hadley's hair and clothing, I could barely look at them. The hurt Maddi wore and the bewildered question she flashed me with her eyes was more than I could take.

"I'm sorry," I mouthed to her as tears spilled onto her cheeks and she moved with the others into the hospital.

CHAPTER 25

I LEANED BACK AGAINST THE AMBULANCE. My head hammered and I couldn't think of what to do next. I wanted to follow them, find out about Hadley, but right now his family probably didn't want me anywhere near. I could only imagine what they thought. I wanted my mom. I felt like a little kid, but I wished she'd come. She'd know what to say, what to do. All I seemed capable of was holding down the blacktop underneath my feet. I doubted Hadley's little sisters had come to the hospital; my mom was probably taking care of them while the rest of his family was with Hadley. We were the neighbors the Bensons knew best.

"Jaxon?"

I lifted my head. Bishop Ward was walking toward me, his face lined with worry. "You okay?"

I nodded, not really sure what to say. Why was he asking about me? "Hadley . . ." I pointed through the glass emergency room doors as if that would tell him all he needed to know.

"I heard," he said. "Brother Spencer's already inside and your dad's on his way over."

For as long as I live, I'll never understand how news can travel through a ward so fast. Part of me was glad the Bensons would have so much support and part of me wished we could all have some time to work this out without the whole world knowing what had happened.

"Should we go in and see how he's doing?" Bishop Ward asked.

My stomach churned. I wasn't sure how I was going to explain everything to the Bensons, but I needed to know about Hadley. Having the bishop there made it a little easier, but I still had a hard time making my feet move.

"It'll be okay," he said, putting his arm around my shoulder and leading me into the hospital.

Brother Spencer wasn't the only one in the waiting room. The Relief Society president, the neighbors on the other side of the Bensons, and a tall man with a plaid shirt and a wide-brimmed hat spoke to each other quietly, all of them with sober expressions. The bishop left me near the group and extended his hand to the man with the hat.

"Pastor Williams," he said as the two men clasped hands.

"Bishop. Glad we could come together on this. It's just a sad ol' mess, isn't it?"

A sad ol' mess. That's exactly what it was. I tried to blend into the stark white walls, hoping nobody would ask questions, listening to them whisper about CT scans and head injuries and *How much more does that family need to take?*

The black-and-white clock on the wall kept ticking, tapping out every minute as I waited and the receptionist clicked her fingernails against the keyboard. She seemed so loud.

Over and over in my head, I ran that stupid race with Bucky—heard the firecrackers go off—saw Hadley so scared. He'd worn his fear, the panic zapping him like an electrical current that wouldn't stop. I saw him running. I saw the tackle. The loud crack of his head played repeatedly in my mind.

It'd only been an hour since Hadley had been hurt, but it felt like a month. Why hadn't anybody come to tell us how he was?

I pushed away from the wall and walked over to the drinking fountain next to the restrooms on the far side of the emergency room—anything to stop the replay. I leaned in for a drink as I pushed the button. I saw my hands again—red, cracked, covered with Hadley's blood. The restroom door felt heavy as I pushed it open and locked it behind me. I ran the water until it was almost scalding and scrubbed until my hands were sore.

I squeezed my eyes shut. All that chaos, and then Hadley had just stopped. That was the worst—the way he was too still.

I dried my hands and slumped to the floor, my back against the door. I just sat there with my knees up, holding my head, my elbows resting on my knees.

"Jax?" It was my dad. "You okay, buddy?"

I didn't answer. I tried to get up but felt rooted to the floor. He knocked.

"I think you'd better come out here," he said.

I finally managed to push myself up and noticed when I opened the door that everybody had quit talking and kind of held their breath. I stepped out and my dad put his arm around my shoulders. I followed his gaze when he turned his head and nodded once. Hadley's dad walked toward us, his shoes rapping the floor with each step. He came through the entrance into the waiting room and slowly scanned the faces of all the people, his expression hard to read, until he found mine.

"Son, can you come with me?"

CHAPTER 26

EVERY MUSCLE IN MY BODY tensed in an instant and a million thoughts crammed my brain. Was I finally going to see Hadley, or was it something else? Maybe more questions from the police. And what would his dad say? Maybe nothing—and that might be worse. I was afraid of what I might find if we went to Hadley's room. What would Hadley's mom say? What would Maddi say? With those thoughts racing through my head, I nodded and forced myself to walk down the hall beside Mr. Benson.

We didn't go far. Hadley was no longer in the emergency room, but he wasn't in a regular hospital room either. The sign posted above the telephone Mr. Benson lifted to ask for admittance read *Critical Care Unit*. It sounded bad when I repeated it in my head.

"Room 143." They were the only words Mr. Benson said. The big double doors opened in slow motion, and we moved through together. The door to Hadley's room was open a crack but Mr. Benson stopped in front of it and turned toward me.

"Hadley's had a couple of seizures, so . . ." He left it at that.

So? So what? The image of Hadley's uncontrollable shuddering against the rocky dirt and then his eerie stillness flashed in my mind. My feet felt too heavy as Mr. Benson pulled open the door and waited for me to walk past.

Hadley lay in the bed, nearly as pale as the sheets, with his eyes closed. He didn't stir as we entered his room. Mrs. Benson stood next to him on the other side of his bed, the one opposite the door, and Maddi sat right next to her with a hand resting protectively on Hadley's arm.

As I moved closer, I still saw blood matted in his hair; flecks of brown dotted his neck and ears. They'd cleaned him up some more, but not all the way. Rather than his stained shirt, the white gown he wore masked most of what had happened. I lifted my eyes and looked at each of the other faces in the room, hoping they'd let me know what I was supposed to do next.

Mrs. Benson smiled a little encouragement and motioned me forward toward Hadley. Maddi's face was blank and unreadable, her eyes red. She didn't even look away from Hadley when I took a step forward.

"He's awake," Mrs. Benson said gently. "Go ahead and talk to him."

But what was I supposed to say?

"Is he . . . okay?" I asked with some serious apprehension at what the answer might be.

"He will be," Mrs. Benson said reassuringly. "The doctors said he has a nasty concussion. He has some stitches, and he was shaken up pretty badly, but they think he'll be good as new."

"I'm so sorry. I never . . ." I wanted to gush apologies, find exactly the right words to make it better, but seeing Hadley again—being in the same room with his family and seeing the worry in their faces—only made the stinging return to my eyes and my voice fail.

"It's okay," Mrs. Benson said with a quiet sincerity. "The officer came and explained." She nodded me forward again. "We'll talk later."

I took a couple of steps, and without opening his eyes, Hadley stuck his right hand through a space in the protective railing as if to shake my hand. I walked forward and took his hand in mine. Instead of his regular enthusiastic shaking, he just held it. His hand was cold and it felt a little uncomfortable to not let go, but I didn't pull away.

"Jaxon-Jaxon Quayle," he said weakly.

"Yeah, buddy, how you feeling?"

He didn't answer right away. I just stood there waiting like Hadley and I were the only two in the room. He lazily opened the eye closest to me.

"Not entirely excellent," he finally answered. "Uh-huh, not excellent."

"I'm so, so sorry," I said. "I never should've run ahead."

"Too loud," he said wincing. "Too, too loud."

"I know. I know." I held his hand harder. Having him talk to me, feeling the tension from his family, even the relief of knowing he was probably going to recover made all the feelings over the day's events surge into my throat, and I had to swallow to make them stay where they belonged. I was so angry— angry at myself, angry at Tanner and Shawn, and, I realized for the first time, angry at Hadley. Why hadn't he left things alone? Why hadn't he just followed us? I knew I was a jerk for thinking any of it was remotely Hadley's fault. It *didn't* think it was Hadley's fault, but I was feeling it anyway, and I was embarrassed.

How was somebody like Tanner ever my friend? I was even embarrassed for the Bensons thinking a move to Burley could be a good thing for them. And I was embarrassed for the ward members in the waiting room. Why would the Bensons want to join a church that had people who would hurt their son? But here was Hadley, asking to see me, holding my hand.

I'd thought I'd been this great guy, that I could be Hadley's friend—his real friend. I couldn't even keep him safe for a couple of hours. I didn't deserve to be his friend.

"Jaxon-Jaxon Quayle," he said, pulling me back from my thoughts.

"Yeah?"

"My head hurts." He said it so matter-of-factly, so . . . normally.

"I know. I'm really sorry," I said the words again, wishing there was a new, better way to say what I felt.

"Perhaps I need a blessing, uh-huh, a blessing through the holy priesthood of God."

What? I immediately turned toward Hadley's parents. They looked as surprised as I probably did. How did he even know about that? They'd been taking the missionary discussions and had gone to church, but I'd been there every time and I didn't remember talking about priesthood blessings in order to be healed. How would his parents feel about it?

The only change I saw in Maddi's expression was a slight narrowing of her eyes.

"You want me to get Pastor Williams, Hadley?" Mr. Benson asked.

Hadley squeezed my hand more firmly than I thought he was capable of. "Jaxon, it is the only true way, the only way to true healing and happiness."

I had no doubt Hadley did not mean Pastor Williams, and I was pretty sure everybody else in the room knew it too. A priesthood blessing for Hadley was right, but just because he'd asked for it didn't mean it was going to happen.

"It has to be okay with your parents," I said.

"Mother," he said weakly. "It is the necessary thing. Uh-huh, very important."

Mrs. Benson gently placed her hand on Hadley's chest and then seemed to ask her husband's permission using only the anxious creases in her face. She softly called his name—"Jeff?"

I shifted uncomfortably as Mr. Benson briefly lifted his eyes to hers and then turned to me, searching my face, stern and intense, as if he squinted hard enough the right answer would appear on my forehead. Hadley closed his eyes again and Maddi's eyes became riveted on me. I barely managed to keep from squirming under all the scrutiny. I shifted my gaze from Mr. Benson to Maddi, hoping I could make her feel how much I wished things had gone differently, but even if she didn't understand at that moment, I knew Hadley needed to have a blessing.

CHAPTER 27

THE LEAVES ON THE TREES were perfectly still, and the air was heavy with heat. I'd never admit it to my mom or dad, but I was glad they'd made me get up early to mow the lawn. The day was only going to get hotter, and this way I'd have time to think without anybody interrupting. I'd already wiped sweat from my forehead more than once and my t-shirt clung to my skin. I appreciated the repetitiveness of walking back and forth across the grass, trying not to repeat the pattern I'd made the last time I'd mowed.

I'd had another nightmare about Hadley's accident, reliving it all again. It would've been nice if he'd jumped out of bed after the priesthood blessing and shouted something like *I'm healed!* but instead he recovered slowly and steadily and seemed more like himself the last week. That helped a lot, but I still couldn't keep my jaw from clenching or the heat from rising into my face when I thought about Tanner and Shawn. Especially Tanner. Good thing I hadn't seen him since the accident.

I glanced at the side of the Bensons' brick house and knew that without the noise of the mower, I'd most likely hear Hadley playing the piano through the open window. I'd been so worried his family would be mad, maybe stop taking the discussions, maybe pack up their stuff and go back to Nebraska. I wouldn't blame them after everything that had happened. But they didn't seem that much different, really—except Maddi.

Last Sunday the missionaries taught the Bensons at our house for the first time since Hadley's accident. Hadley again backed up principles the missionaries taught by quoting the Bible and even using a few verses from the Book of Mormon. I was surprised how all of the kids participated; even my brother Jarom had something to say. Mrs. Benson wore a calm, even smile the whole time and asked a couple of great questions about the Atonement. Mr. Benson barely said a word, which I realized now was part of his personality, but he still seemed to take an interest in what they were teaching. Maddi acted like she was listening but it was clear she was uncomfortable. She was quieter and often had at least her fingers resting lightly on Hadley's arm or shoulder, often distracted by watching him. We'd barely spoken since the accident and I didn't think talking to her about it in a room full of people was the best choice.

Maybe later I'd ask if she and Hadley wanted to go for the ice cream I'd promised him at the golf course on the Fourth of July. Hopefully she'd agree and we could talk then.

I didn't notice Mrs. Benson standing by the fence until I changed directions with the mower and faced her. She wore dirty gardening gloves on her hands, which rested on the top rail. I smiled nervously when she motioned me over. I killed the engine and walked to meet her.

"Hey, Jaxon," she said.

"Hi." I waited while she seemed to gather her thoughts.

"We haven't really had a chance to talk," she said.

I wanted to say that was okay with me but instead I shrugged a shoulder and nodded, trying to act relaxed.

"I guess I wanted to say thank you," she said.

Thank you? She must have recognized the confused look on my face.

"The past year and a half hasn't been easy," she said with a faraway look, as if she was recalling each of the difficult events one by one.

Sorry didn't seem good enough. I stood quietly, wondering how many of those events I'd contributed to.

"No," she said gently. "You have no reason to apologize. None of this has been your fault. Things happen."

"But—" I broke in, feeling an unexpected lump form in my throat and having the urge to point out all of the reasons she was wrong.

"No *buts*, Jaxon. Can you imagine how hard it must've been for Maddi to switch high schools in the middle of her junior year, especially after just losing—" her voice caught and I waited while she swallowed hard—"losing her brother? She never once complained to us, but I'm sure she shed some tears into her pillow. We knew it would be her helping Hadley through this transition too. We had no idea whether he'd be accepted. And, true, not everybody's learned to love him as much as the rest of us—"

I'm pretty sure we were both thinking about Tanner.

"But you've been such a good friend to both of them and I'm so grateful. We'll just have to do our best to try to understand the others—and forgive them."

She paused, maybe letting her words sink in. I felt my stomach tighten. *Forgive Tanner?* I couldn't. I couldn't just forgive and forget. Not Tanner. Not yet. And how could *she*?

"Hadley's not always . . . easy." She chuckled and then continued. "Anyway, Maddi's carried a lot of extra weight and you've helped her more than I think you realize."

I shifted uncomfortably. Tanner had been more than a jerk. He'd been stupid and mean. But how many times had I walked away from some awkward Hadley situation? If she only knew the truth—how frustrated I'd been with both Maddi and Hadley or how hard it was for me to understand why Maddi would spend so much time with him. I hoped Mrs. Benson would confuse the color I felt moving up my neck for humility instead of guilt.

"You've stuck by them, Jaxon, and next to Maddi, Hadley considers you his very best friend."

"He thinks everybody's his friend," I said before thinking.

"Pretty much," she acknowledged with a laugh. "But not like you," she continued more seriously. "I know it's not a very manly thing to say, but Hadley loves you."

I lowered my eyes. I realized, maybe for the first time, that I felt the same about him too, and it surprised me. *But what about Maddi?* I wanted to ask. And then, just like it was their queue to enter, Hadley and Maddi walked out the front door and across the lawn to where Mrs. Benson and I stood.

"My very good friend Jaxon-Jaxon Quayle."

"Hey, buddy."

We shook hands even though we both wore gloves for working in the yard.

"Hey, Maddi," I said, noticing how tan her summer skin was and how big her eyes looked with her hair pulled into two loose braids.

"Hi, Jaxon," she said and then turned to her mom. "We're all ready to help. Where do you want us?"

"Maybe you two could work out here in the flower beds and I'll get back to pulling weeds in the garden. Are the girls on their way out? I thought I'd have them help me."

"Should be," Maddi said. "They were just finishing up their cereal and toast."

"Well, then, let's get started," Mrs. Benson said. "It was nice talking to you, Jaxon."

"Thanks," I said sincerely with one nod of my head. I thought I caught a quick flash of curiosity flit across Maddi's face before she turned with Hadley toward the beds running along the sidewalk leading to their front door.

"Hey," I called before any of them had gotten far. "You guys want to go for ice cream later? I still owe Hadley. If it's okay with you, Mrs. Benson."

"Excellent idea, uh-huh. Excellent solution for the celebration," Hadley interrupted. "Pralines and cream in a cup. Double scoop or possibly a triple for special occasions."

Maddi and Mrs. Benson lifted their eyebrows at the same time.

Mrs. Benson walked back toward Hadley and Maddi. "I thought you wanted to keep it a surprise," she said in a secretive tone as she leaned in to Hadley.

I looked from Maddi to her mom. "Am I missing something?" I asked. "What're we celebrating? Somebody's birthday?"

"You better tell him now, Hadley," Mrs. Benson said.

The closest I'd seen to a smile on him broke out across his face. "Baptism for the Bensons, uh-huh, the Benson family baptism, exactly one week, five hours, and thirty minutes from now. One o'clock p.m.," he said. "Can't be late. Never be late."

"Seriously?"

Mrs. Benson grinned and nodded.

"That's awesome!" Before I knew it, I'd jumped the three-rail fence and stood shaking Hadley's hand hard enough to compete with his. "The Benson family baptism. Sounds like the name of a movie. I like it! The whole family? I bet the elders are excited."

Mrs. Benson's smile faltered, and she moved toward Maddi, putting her arm around her shoulder almost protectively. I stopped shaking Hadley's hand.

"Almost the whole family," she said. Maddi dropped her chin and twisted the ring on her finger.

CHAPTER 28

THERE WAS NO GOOD WAY to ask the questions I wanted to ask. *Why* not *the whole family?* Maddi, it seemed, had made another decision. But why? *She had to know the gospel was true. Didn't she?* And was her decision final? Some of the Bensons were getting baptized, right? It was a start. But I felt like I'd been punched in the stomach. *Why* not *Maddi?*

And then I thought about the Fourth of July and Hadley's accident. That's when things had changed. Maddi had changed. I guess maybe I had too. We hadn't had a real conversation for weeks, even when I'd gone to visit Hadley after he'd come home from the hospital. I guess I'd been too nervous about what she thought or what she might say; she'd seemed to be avoiding me too. Hadley had probably needed even more attention than usual—but still, standing in the Bensons' yard, I wondered if Maddi not getting baptized with the rest of her family had anything to do with me—if there was something I could've done differently. I wished I would've talked to her sooner.

We stood awkwardly, as though none of us knew what to say exactly. *Sorry* didn't seem like the right thing. *Congratulations* felt wrong too. I was relieved when Mrs. Benson offered some help.

"Maddi and her father have decided to wait for a while," she said. "And of course little Chloe, although we may have to hog-tie her to keep her from jumping in."

I grinned politely.

"It's okay. It's fine," Hadley added. "Maybe later. uh-huh. Jeffery A. Benson, my father, along with Madelyn Kaye Benson just need time—time to think and ponder."

The door wasn't completely closed, then.

"Well . . . okay," I said with a grin and as much sincerity as I could muster. "I guess they'd better have some time, then."

What else could I say?

Maddi's shoulders seemed to relax. She glanced up and met my eyes for a brief moment. Her small grin felt a little easier and I smiled back even though I didn't feel very happy. *Why was I taking this so personally?* I wondered.

I was on the Bensons' side of the fence and still needed to finish mowing my lawn, but I hesitated, hoping one of the Bensons would shout out *Just kidding!* and then tell me the family baptism included all of them.

It didn't happen.

"Thanks for letting me know about . . . everything," I said. "I really think it's awesome."

I walked toward the fence and put my shoe on the rail to hop over. I didn't look back to see if they were still standing there, staring at the back of my head, or had gone to do their own chores. I wanted to get back to the monotony and let my thoughts unwind.

The mower started after only the second pull. I watched the ground while I tugged the handle in the opposite direction, making sure to face away from the Bensons while I walked, even if it meant re-mowing part of the lawn.

Right from the start, I'd had a thing for Maddi. How could I not? I thought about the first day I'd seen her. Even after traveling for who knew how long, she was beautiful. Now, though, there was more to it. It wasn't just that she was pretty. I *liked* her. I liked how she laughed, that she read books I never wanted to read, and that she could dominate at soccer. I liked that she didn't wear makeup if she didn't want to, loved her family so much, and treated other people, no matter who they were, like they mattered. I wanted her to get baptized because it was right—because she was the best member of the Church I knew and she wasn't even a member.

Before Hadley got hurt she was almost there. I knew it. I felt it. I pushed the mower toward the fence again. Maybe Hadley's mom and sisters could forgive what had happened, but Maddi was closer to Hadley than anybody. *I* was struggling to forgive, and Hadley wasn't my twin brother.

I turned back toward the Bensons' house. Maddi knelt with her back to me, next to Hadley, digging in the dirt. I turned the mower off.

"Maddi, can I talk to you?" My voice sounded shallow after the buzz of the mower. Maddi sat back, but didn't answer. I almost asked again, thinking maybe she hadn't heard me, when she looked over her shoulder. She hesitated, seeming to weigh her decision, and finally stood, pulling off her gloves and laying them in the dirt of the flower bed.

"Hadley, could you go help Mom for a while? I need to talk to Jaxon for a minute, okay?"

"However I have a very important question, an urgent request for my very good friend Jaxon-Jaxon Quayle."

"And you can ask him as soon as we're finished talking," Maddi said. "We shouldn't take too long. I bet Mom and the girls could use your big muscles out back."

Hadley darted a sharp glance at Maddi and then another at his biceps, flexing. I had to hide my chuckle when the flattery worked and he trudged without another word to the backyard.

As soon as Maddi faced me, the temperature of the already-hot air seemed to rise another ten degrees.

"Do you mind if we sit in the shade?" she asked. "I'm melting."

I could've kissed her. Well . . . maybe not yet.

We moved under the cool of the big leafed tree in the middle of the Bensons' front yard and sat cross-legged on the ground across from each other. I pulled off my gloves while Maddi plucked blades of grass and heaped them in a pile.

"I know it's not really any of my business," I said, automatically leaning in when I rested my elbows on my knees, letting my hands fall loosely between them. "But I'm going to ask anyway." I took a deep breath. "What's up, Maddi? Why aren't you getting baptized?"

She looked at me for a second then went back to picking grass.

"I'm not sure how to explain," she said, pausing long enough that I doubted my decision to ask.

"You don't have to say anything," I offered. "Like I said, it's not really any of my business."

Even though I really wanted to know what she thought, she didn't seem willing to answer. "It's okay," I said and started to get up.

"Wait," she said, grasping my wrist. "It's probably as much your business as mine. You're the reason I agreed to listen to the missionaries in the first place."

Really?

"And don't pretend you're surprised," she said lightly.

But I was. It was Heather who had invited her.

"Do you know how many people there are in Pickrell?" she asked.

What did this have to do with anything? I shook my head slowly.

"No idea," I said.

"If Mr. Moore's still alive, just more than a hundred and eighty, minus the Benson family. Our whole town could fit in your chapel with room to spare."

This time I nodded. *Okay . . .*

"Technically, Pickrell isn't a town; it's a village," she continued. "It doesn't even have a mayor. But everybody seems so proud to be from there, like there's something secretly special about it. As cliché as it might sound, we were like a big family."

She looked off into the distance like she could see the whole town and everybody in it right in front of her.

"I still miss it like crazy," she said. "Almost everybody farmed and in the early fall we'd all get together at the park by the creek and have a giant picnic to celebrate the harvest. I looked forward to it every year." She met my gaze with a grin. "Cheesy, huh?"

"It sounds . . . cool," I said.

"It was. Our family always got invited to the Lutheran church socials too. They always had the best food. I'm pretty sure we were the only Baptists in town, but the Lutherans seemed to think it was only a matter of time. They were such good people—but we were *Baptists*, you know?"

I didn't really.

"We drove into Beatrice every Sunday for church," she continued. "And again during the week so James, Hadley, and I could go to our youth group. Amanda—my best friend—and I went to the same congregation our entire lives. So did my boyf—"

She paused and that familiar color flooded her cheeks.

"Your boyfriend," I finished for her. Of course she'd had a boyfriend. She was awesome. Maddi had this whole other life she'd had to leave behind. In my mind, as far as the Bensons were concerned, there was Burley and there was pre-Burley—I never knew any details other than the ones that might filter through the conversation. I suddenly felt like the most self-centered person in the universe. Why hadn't I ever asked about it? "What's his name?"

She hesitated, but when I held her eyes with encouragement, she answered, "Justin." She said it quietly with a smile but it was a sad smile. "We broke up before our family moved. I didn't think it was fair.

"I guess what I'm trying to say is that joining a different church is a big deal for me and for my family. The people from the only church in town had worked on us for years and it didn't change how we felt. Then we came to Burley and, well . . ." She chuckled. "We'd been warned about the Mormons, you know. We thought we might have dodged a bullet coming to Idaho instead of Utah, but leave it to us to move right next door to the LDS poster family."

"Should I be offended?" I asked jokingly but then continued more seriously. "If things were so great in Pickrell, why'd you leave?"

"Even before James died our farm was struggling with the competition from the big commercial farms. And when the economy fell apart, we were barely hanging on. My dad started looking for another job—not too seriously in the beginning—but I don't think it helped that the memory of James was everywhere. I couldn't imagine what it was like for my dad to work in the same field where James died, having to relive every day the horror of finding him. We all missed him so much. Still do. And then a job offer came. At first he didn't really consider it, thinking there was no way the farm would sell, but it did. Our neighbors must've figured we'd made some deal with the devil, selling to one of the bigger farmers in the area, but it was that or lose everything. I think my parents saw the sale as confirmation that moving was the right thing to do."

"What did you think?" I asked.

She took a breath. "I was afraid to leave Nebraska. Everything I knew was there, but a part of me was excited to try something new. I worried about Hadley. He doesn't always do so well with change, but I thought we could work it out together. Having to say good-bye was one of the hardest things I've ever had to do, especially to James, but once I did and the boxes were packed, I thought I was ready."

"Were you?"

She bit her bottom lip and then answered. "That's the thing. There have been so *many* changes—losing James, leaving my friends, leaving the farm. . . . I *thought* I was doing okay but maybe I'm not as brave as I thought. Moving to a different school and being the new girl has been hard. Trying to figure out how to fit in or if I even wanted to was just as hard."

I'd never thought of *fitting in* as a choice. You either did or didn't. I thought she'd done pretty well.

"And trying to help Hadley through the same things," she continued. "I think he was doing better than I was until Shawn and Tanner." Her jaw tensed and she looked away. "Why would they do something like that?"

I rested my hand on her knee and she met my gaze, the hurt pooling in her eyes.

"I'm so sorry," I said. "I've wished a thousand times I would've done things differently that day. I never would've left Hadley. It was so obvious that Tanner and Shawn were up to something, but I never thought they'd . . ." I shook my head and felt the familiar anger welling up. "No wonder you don't want to get baptized. How could anybody blame you? We've all done such a great job representing the Church," I said bitterly.

"That's exactly how I felt," she said. "There was no way I'd be baptized into a church where Tanner was a member. I'd felt totally justified when the missionaries asked and I'd said no." Then her face relaxed and she gently grinned. "But then I thought about you and it completely messed up my reasoning. You're good, Jaxon and you're a member of the same church Tanner is." She put her hand on top of mine. "None of this is your fault—not what happened to Hadley and not me waiting to be baptized. I just need time to work through some things with God."

I envied the matter-of-fact way she seemed to know how to *work through some things with God*—like she was just waiting for their appointment and then it would happen.

"I'm sort of jealous about how the rest of my family seems so sure," Maddi said. "Daddy would probably join now too if he wasn't protecting me from being the Lone Ranger in this whole thing. I guess I need to be sure joining your church is the right thing at the right time for me." She pulled another hand full of grass. "That, and I'm not so sure I'm big enough to forgive yet. I need to work on it."

I knew what she meant. I couldn't even think about Tanner and Shawn without wanting to break something. I didn't know what else to say, but I got it. Maddi had said she didn't think she was brave but she was. I probably would've been baptized with the rest of my family just because they were getting baptized. I felt the warmth of her hand on mine and before I even thought about it, I leaned forward and kissed her on the cheek.

I pulled away slowly, not sure what to expect, but Maddi just said, "Thanks." She seemed to mean it.

We both jumped when Hadley poked his head around the side of the house and half-shouted, "Jaxon-Jaxon Quayle."

"What can I say? He has great timing," Maddi said.

I stood and offered a hand to pull her up, and she moved beside me.

"I think you had a question," I said to Hadley.

"Yes, a very important question. Uh-huh. Urgent and significant," Hadley said while walking toward us with long, wooden, yet determined strides. He took one step too many and stopped. I inched backwards until there was more space between us as he seemed to study the space on the ground next to my feet, but he didn't ask his question.

"Okay," I said. "I'm ready."

He darted one of his quick glances at me. "Uh-huh. One week, four hours, and three minutes until the Benson family baptism," he said. "Benson family minus Madelyn Kaye, Jeffery Alan, and Chloe Jane."

What was with the middle names?

"Yep, I know," I said, stealing a glance at Maddi. She looked as curious as I felt.

Hadley nodded once.

"Very important," he said, barely rocking at his waist but then stopping and seeming to stand taller. "It would be an honor, uh-huh, an honor and a privilege if my very good friend Jaxon-Jaxon Bentley Quayle—"

Bentley? Maddi mouthed. "This must be important, Hadley. You're being so formal."

"If Jaxon Quayle," he repeated, "would consent to baptize Hadley-Hadley Benson a member of The Church of Jesus Christ of Latter-day Saints."

Maddi raised her eyebrows in surprise.

"Me?" I swallowed. It didn't seem that long ago I'd knelt in front of the font to watch older cousins or kids from Primary get baptized. "I've never done it before," I answered, feeling new sweat bead on my forehead.

"A-Okay," Hadley said. "Just fine. Have to start at the very beginning. Uh-huh, everyone must start someplace."

But I'd only been a priest for a few months. What if I wasn't ready? What if I messed up? This was Hadley we were talking about, and I had to be honest; I could think of about a hundred things that could go wrong. Did he even like water? Hadley stood firm. I looked to Maddi for help, but she only shrugged. I shifted my gaze when Chloe bounded from the backyard, followed by the rest of the Benson girls—including Mrs. Benson.

"Did he say yeth?" Chloe shouted through the gap where he front teeth had been. I looked from face to face; each of them wore an expectant grin.

"No pressure," Maddi said.

My short life with Hadley flashed before my eyes—him wanting me to shake his hand and carry a box at the same time, him playing the organ at church, him almost killing half the people at the golf course. And then I pictured him in the hospital, his hand stretched out to me through the metal bars. How could I say no? I crouched down to Chloe's level.

"Yep," I directed to her. "He said yeth."

Then I turned and looked only at Hadley. "It would be *my* honor and privilege to baptize you," I said.

He paused to peek at Maddi and then his mother. They each grinned and then Hadley and I shook on it.

"Excellent," he said. "Most outstanding."

CHAPTER 29

You can't be serious, I THOUGHT when Tanner pushed away from the wall he'd obviously been leaning against near the entrance of the church. I wanted to pretend I hadn't seen him and find another way in, but it was too late.

"Jaxon," he said.

I paused and noticed he was wearing a shirt and tie.

"What are you doing here?" I asked, my shoulders tightening instantly. I probably shouldn't punch him right before baptizing Hadley, but I wanted to.

"I came to talk to you," he said. "And they invited me—the Bensons."

What? I didn't believe it. Why would they invite him after what he'd done?

"I need to get in there and get ready," I said. "I don't want to be late."

Never be late, I heard Hadley say in my head.

"I just need a minute."

Tanner shifted and I noticed he bit the inside of his bottom lip, something I hadn't seen him do before.

"All right. What?" I said tersely.

He hesitated and then took a deep breath and blew out quickly through his mouth. "I've practiced what I was going to say a hundred times, but it's a lot harder with you actually standing here."

I stared at him silently, giving him nothing.

"Okay, I guess all I can say is I'm sorry. I've been a jerk."

"Yeah, you have."

Maybe I should've been the bigger person and told him it was fine, but I couldn't. Which was worse, being ticked off or lying?

"Okay, well, I just wanted you to know."

Where was the usual cockiness in his voice? He reached for the handle on the door and pulled.

"Wait, did you think you could just say you were sorry and it would make everything better?" I asked before he walked through. "Really?"

He turned back around and stood squarely in front of me.

"No. I didn't," he said. "But I thought it was a start. You know, I thought it was going to be so much harder apologizing to the whole Benson family. All of them were there last night, but they were a lot easier than you. What can I do, Jaxon? How can I fix it? I'd really like to know, because I feel like crap every day."

"Good," I said, not about to cut him any slack, even though I had to admit it took guts to apologize to their entire family.

Tanner ducked his head. I told myself the hurt on his face couldn't be real. It didn't fit his profile.

"You were *laughing* at the golf course," I said. "You thought your plans were so funny. What did you think was going to happen?"

He looked up.

"Do you really want to know?" he asked.

I realized I did.

"Yeah."

"I wanted the dog crap to get all over your stuff. Yours. And maybe Bucky's too. It was perfect, you guys running for the river. We set off the fire crackers, thinking we'd hide and watch until you found the mess and then get out of there. We thought it'd be hilarious." He shook his head. "We didn't know Hadley was going to turn around and come back. How could we?"

I replayed the day in my head and had to admit that what he was saying could be true. Maybe he wasn't targeting Hadley, exactly, but it still didn't make it okay.

"What about all of the other times—at the soccer game? At school? At church? Why Hadley?"

He rubbed his chin with his fingers. "I knew it bugged you," he said. "It sounds stupid saying it out loud, but I guess I was jealous."

"Jealous of what?" But I already knew—at least part of it. "Maddi?"

Tanner didn't answer, but I saw him clench, staring hard at some random spot on the ground.

"Really," I said, kind of amazed. "You'd do that to somebody like Hadley because his sister *maybe* liked somebody else? Wow. How did that work for you? Does she like you now?"

"You know what?" Tanner blurted. "Everybody thinks you're so cool and you don't even care. Bucky, too. You know what it's like trying to compete with that? I finally beat you to it when I asked Maddi to prom and you still ended up taking her home. I wanted to hurt *you*. I'm not proud of it, but it's the truth, even if I feel like an idiot saying it."

He blew out a fast breath and we stared at each other without saying anything. I wanted to stay mad. He deserved it. But instead, I felt sorry for him.

"You were right," I said. "It bothered me. I was angry and felt stupid that somebody I thought was my friend would do those things, but you didn't hurt me nearly as much as you hurt Hadley or Maddi or the rest of the Bensons. They didn't deserve it and you're lucky they're better people than either one of us."

Tanner swallowed hard and nodded his head, slowly.

I looked away, toward the door, and noticed Hadley's face inches from the glass. He pushed it open and poked his head out.

"12:33 p.m.," he said. "Not a moment to spare, uh-huh. Time's a wastin', Grandma Benson says."

"I'm coming right now," I said and then turned to look at Tanner. "You asked what you could do to fix things?"

"Yeah?" he asked intently.

"Be his friend," I answered and then followed Hadley into the building.

I had no idea so many people would be there. We were supposed to start in the Primary room where the font was, but so many people had come to support the Benson family that the missionaries, the Bensons, and I craned our necks from the front row of the chapel to listen to the bishop conduct from the pulpit. Maddi and her dad sat on the same row as the rest of us, but Mr. Benson wore a dark suit, Chloe a pink dress, and Maddi a light yellow skirt with a blue top in contrast to our white jumpsuits. The meeting had started late, but it had nothing to do with me or my talk with Tanner. Hadley wouldn't sit down until he'd shaken every person's hand in the room. I was so tense I could barely remember the opening exercises or moving into the other room when the time came.

Hadley and I stepped into the font together—not exactly a hot tub, but warm enough. Hadley clung to the rail with both hands and stopped before reaching the last step that would take him all the way in.

I glanced around nervously at everybody in the room—my family, the Bensons, Bucky, Tanner, and Tanner's dad, standing at the back—and then moved in front of Hadley, speaking quietly.

"We're going to be okay," I said, trying to reassure both of us. "We can do this."

He put his back against the rail, still holding on with one hand and cradling his stomach with the other arm. He rocked silently, causing ripples in the water. It seemed everybody in the room held their breath together and I wondered what would happen if Hadley suddenly freaked out. At least there'd be other people to help this time. I understood his anxiety, though. My hands were shaking too.

He paused and then stepped down. I tentatively took hold of his arm with my hand.

"It's all right," I said. "Nice and easy, remember? Just like we talked about. Close your eyes, plug your nose, and hold on tight. All the way under. You ready?"

He did as I asked, but then opened one eye and placed his hand on my forearm like I'd shown him in a picture. I raised my other arm to the square.

"Here we go," I said. "You all right?"

Hadley didn't flinch. I was touching him, and not just shaking his hand. He didn't push me away. I stole a quick glance at Maddi, and she smiled with understanding.

"My very good friend Jaxon-Jaxon Quayle," he said with his eyes still closed. "Won't let go, uh-huh, never let go."

"Nope. Won't let go, buddy. Promise."

ABOUT THE AUTHOR

JODY WIND DURFEE OFTEN HIKES the craggy mountains just outside the front door of a house where she lives with her husband, children, and three red hens. She's been known to randomly break out into song and has a deep, abiding love for chocolate chip cookies. When she's not enraptured by her favorite book of the week, she coaches Special Olympics and enjoys the impromptu concerts given by her children and her friends. *Hadley-Hadley Benson* is her debut novel.